The Stalker
Paperback Copyright © 2022 Lorhainne Ekelund
Editor: Talia Leduc

ISBN-13: 9781998775231

Give feedback on the book at:
lorhainneeckhart@hotmail.com

Twitter: @LEckhart
Facebook: AuthorLorhainneEckhart

Printed in the U.S.A

The Stalker

THE O'CONNELLS
BOOK THIRTEEN

LORHAINNE ECKHART

The O'Connells of Livingston, Montana, are not your typical family. Follow them on their journey to the dark and dangerous side of love in a series of romantic thrillers you won't want to miss. Raised by a single mother after their father's mysterious disappearance eighteen years ago, the six grown siblings live in a small town with all kinds of hidden secrets, lies, and deception. Much like the contemporary family romance series focusing on the Friessens, this romantic suspense series follows the lives of the O'Connell family as each of the siblings searches for love.

The O'Connells

The Neighbor
The Third Call
The Secret Husband
The Quiet Day
The Commitment, An O'Connell Novella
The Missing Father
The Hometown Hero
Justice
The Family Secret
The Fallen O'Connell
The Return of the O'Connells
And The She Was Gone
The Stalker
The O'Connell Family Christmas
The Girl Next Door
Broken Promises
The Gatekeeper
The Hunted

A small-town girl who's a bit of a misfit. The perfect guy who's anything but. Will his suspicious behavior reveal things she doesn't want to know?

Alison Sweetgrass-O'Connell believes she's forever a misfit and will never fit in.

After struggling to recover from a teenage crush that dealt her a crippling blow, Alison watches from the sidelines in the small town of Livingston, Montana, which hasn't been friendly to her. Silently, she believes everyone's seemingly perfect lives have a dark side. And soon her beliefs prove true.

Alison meets young, attractive med student Bennett Warren, new to Livingston. Suddenly, Bennett is showing up everywhere she is—and then, in her good fortune, he turns out to have rented the apartment right next door.

At first, she's convinced it's fate, and maybe there is hope for her, but a suspicious turn of events has her fearing she's being stalked by someone who knows one of her secrets, something no one should know.
She tries telling herself she's imagining things, but she soon realizes someone has been inside her apartment, going through her very personal belongings. She finds herself looking over her shoulder, not knowing who she can trust. When she confides in Bennett, she's convinced he thinks she's crazy, too.

Then Alison comes across evidence that has her questioning not only her sanity but also the real reason Bennett showed up in Livingston—and even more disturbing is the possibility that him moving right next door to her wasn't entirely coincidental.

CHAPTER
One

Did anyone else slip out of bed in the morning planning to kill someone?

As Alison stared at the list of names in her journal, she underlined Belinda Lee's again in red, picturing her perfect smile, perfect body. Belinda wrapped every guy around her finger, and every one of them had believed everything she'd said. She'd thrown Alison under the bus with lies and more lies to save her own skin.

It seemed her entire life had been a series of people believing she was an easy target, a scapegoat who would never fight back.

Her pen hovered over the page again. She had to remind herself that Cassie Arnold—scratch that, Cassie Baker—shouldn't be on the list. She crossed out her name and then circled the two columns, which contained the names of everyone who had hurt her with lies and stories, targeting her just because of who she was: someone who could never fit in.

But Cassie had never done that. Her only crime had been falling in love with Brady.

There was a knock at her bedroom door, and she closed the red hardcover book and shoved it in her bedside table just as the door opened. There was her dad, Ryan. She wondered whether she would still feel like she did now, as if life was against her, if she'd been raised by him instead of Wren, a man who'd loved her but hated her mother.

He had been twisted, sick—likely why she was the freak she struggled not to be today.

"You could wait until I say to come in, you know," she told him, wondering if sarcasm and nastiness dripped from her voice.

Her dad raised a brow, and then there was a tug at his lips. Of course, he was fighting some amusement at her expense. "Then you'd never answer," he said. "Figured you were either sleeping or ignoring the world. I see it's the latter. Everything okay, kiddo?"

There it was, the fatherly concern she had to remind herself was normal. He lingered in the doorway, his hand on the frame, dressed in his ranger uniform, already packing his gun.

"Fine," she said. "Why wouldn't it be?"

Oh, maybe the fact that she was still stuck in her misery since seeing Belinda Lee just the day before. She had walked into the Bluebird, the bustling restaurant Alison had worked her ass off at for the past year, doing all the shit jobs to try to get the coveted evening waitress position, where the tips were high and the hourly pay was a dollar more. Belinda had walked in and landed the job after just five minutes with the manager. It had been just one more kick to the head.

"I thought you and I could snag breakfast together this morning and talk and catch up," Ryan said. "Your mom is across the street with Charlotte. The two of them are working on Marcus's campaign."

Right, her uncle was running to keep his job as sheriff. It seemed her dad was ready to poke his nose into her business.

"I'm not really hungry," she said. "I have work." *In six hours.*

Her dad angled his head and stared at her with those deep O'Connell blue eyes. He seemed at times to know what she was thinking and feeling. But maybe that was just her imagination. He didn't move or look away, though.

"Pretty sure you work the dinner shift," he said. "It was a big deal last week when you no longer had to work the breakfast and lunch crowd for a pittance, as you put it, of tips. You're in the big leagues now. Or has something changed? Are you back working the early shift?" He crossed his arms as he leaned against the doorframe with seemingly no intention of walking away.

She tried to figure out what to say. She didn't much like being caught in a lie, and she wished her grandma were around to talk to and just make her feel better. But she was just someone else who had left her.

"Fine," Alison said. "But I'm not ready to eat breakfast. It's too early."

"Nonsense," Ryan said. "Get dressed. Breakfast is the most important meal of the day." He gestured toward her as he took a step past the doorway. She knew she was frowning, but he didn't seem to notice. "We haven't had much time to talk, and it's time to check in, since you haven't been around for family night this week. If left to your own devices and given space, you'd continue to be stuck in your head, miserable, gathering enough rope to hang yourself, as I can see from your face now." He glanced to his watch and then back to her. "Say, ten minutes, downstairs. I'll warm the truck."

"What? Wait, you mean we're going out?" Now she was sitting straight up, alarm tightening her chest. She was wearing a baggy nightshirt on her messy bed, and her image in the dresser mirror revealed bed hair and unwashed makeup from the night before.

"Yeah, breakfast out," he said. "You have time. We'll talk, catch up, and you can tell me everything that's going on in that head of yours. Namely, you can explain why I'm hearing second-hand that you applied for an apartment rental at the Carlyle and didn't bother saying anything to your mom and me. So come on, get up, and clean up and get dressed. You have ten minutes. See you downstairs." Then her dad tapped the door frame and was gone, walking away.

She listened to the creak on the stairs, a sinking feeling in her stomach as she said, under her breath, "Shit."

"Yeah, I heard that," Ryan called out. "Ten minutes, Alison. Get your butt in gear."

She wondered now how much more he was listening to when she thought he wasn't. As she climbed from bed, she was stuck on one question: How had he found out about her applying to rent an apartment? She hadn't told anyone when she spotted the for-rent sign, called the number, and filled out an application that didn't include her parents' names for references, yet he seemed to know even though she had yet to hear back from the building manager about whether her application had been approved.

Right, just one more person who was messing with her.

"You know there's no shortage of restaurants," she said. "Did you have to bring me to the place I work?"

At least they were in a corner. She fought the urge to run her fingers through her wet hair, which was still damp from the quick shower she'd grabbed. She'd thrown on white sweatpants and a matching bulky and comfortable hoodie, and when she'd finally gone downstairs, her dad had been standing at the bottom, checking his watch.

"Hey, stop complaining, considering I'm the one who had to wait for you," Ryan said. "When I said ten minutes, I didn't mean for you to take a twenty-minute shower and then try on everything in your room while I waited downstairs. I thought you'd throw something on, brush your teeth, wash your face, and we'd go."

Alison reached for a packet of sugar and tapped it before ripping it open to pour into the steaming coffee Nan had brought as soon as they sat down. Nan was the waitress who had trained her, an older woman close to retirement, with hair she'd let go pure white and a smile that always warmed her. She'd reminded Alison that customers liked a happy waitress, not one with a chip on her shoulder. She stirred in the sugar and then tapped her spoon on the edge of her mug, fighting the urge to roll her shoulders, very aware that her boss, Chad Hargrave—older, married, and balding—was walking their way.

"It wasn't twenty minutes," she said. "I'm not a guy, who can get out of bed and throw on the first thing he sees. I'm a girl. It takes me more than ten minutes to get ready."

She didn't have to look up to know that Chad was now standing there, but she lifted her mug to drink as she took in the man who had welcomed Belinda with open arms.

"Hey there, Alison," Chad said. "Listen, we're kind of short staffed, so I need you to start earlier today. Then I'm going to put you back on the lunch shift for the rest of the week. Okay?" He patted her back and smiled at her dad, then didn't wait for a response before walking away.

She felt her jaw slacken, her appetite disappearing, and she squeezed the handle of her mug, firming her lips, wondering how that had just happened.

"Why didn't you speak up?" Ryan said.

She dragged her gaze back to her dad, who lifted his mug, took a swallow of coffee, and then closed up the laminate menu and slid it to the edge of the table.

"And say what, no?" She could feel her attitude with a dash of anger. Why did she feel as if there was a "Kick me" sign taped to her back?

"Well, for starters, didn't you say the dinner shift is what you wanted?" Ryan said. "You make more tips there, but now you're suddenly working a shift you don't want again. When you work for someone, you don't have a lot of say, but you do have a voice. If you don't speak up, you'll get walked over. So is this a permanent demotion? Just saying, you have to use your words and talk and communicate instead of going right to that place of having a chip on your shoulder and being angry at the world."

She rested her elbows on the table, holding her coffee mug between both hands. Nan was running plates out from the back, wearing blue jeans and a faded blue shirt. The breakfast and lunch crowd were casual, but for the dinner shift, they were a little more on the dressy side.

"I don't have a chip on my shoulder, but he's my boss," Alison said. "I'm pretty sure if I said no, the next thing he'd say is 'Pick up your check. You're fired.'"

She wasn't sure what to make of the amusement in her dad's expression as he shook his head and said, "Now you're being overdramatic. Words matter, and you have to speak up. Talking isn't your strong suit, I know. You hold things in, Alison. You get pissed off and think the world is out to get you, but it isn't. What you give out is what you get back. Well, at least you can show up for family night now, and we can keep tabs on you again, check in and find out what you're doing, talk…you know, like families do. And maybe you can explain why you're suddenly renting an apartment and moving out."

She took a swallow of the bitter coffee that needed something else, more sugar, maybe cream. She put the mug down on the table. "It's called being an adult. It's time to have my own life and place. I didn't know I'd been approved to rent the apartment. I applied and was told they'd get back to me. So how did you find out?"

She wondered for a moment if her dad would answer her question. He glanced over to the side as Nan hurried past and said, "I'll be right back to take your order!"

Ryan pulled in a breath and leaned back, nodding. "Being eighteen doesn't make you an adult," he said. "There aren't many people I don't know in this town, and since you didn't put any references down on your application, my phone was suddenly ringing. I went to school with Trish Huckman, who manages the Carlyle. She was wondering why you signed the application as Alison Sweetgrass, not O'Connell. Everyone in this town knows you're my daughter, but you're still using Wren's last name? I don't like the kinds of questions that raises. As you know, people create problems that aren't there. They come up with their own version of the truth."

She had hesitated, since she usually wrote Sweetgrass-O'Connell. She had even wondered, for a moment, if he'd understand.

"A habit, I guess," she replied. "I didn't think it was a big deal."

She stared at her coffee. Sometimes letting a lie roll off

her tongue was easier than explaining why she did the things she did. When she flicked her gaze back to her dad, he was staring at her and leaning back, and his blue eyes held an edge of hurt. Okay, now she felt like shit.

"It is a big deal, Alison," he said. "You're my daughter…" He let out a sigh, and she knew he was taking it personally. "Alison Sweetgrass-O'Connell is your name. You're an O'Connell. Or do you have a problem with being my daughter? I thought we were past this."

She didn't know what to say. She wished she could go back and undo that moment and write her full name. Wren hadn't exactly been father of the year, yet she was still holding on to that piece of him even though she would never walk away from her family here.

"No, Dad, there isn't. You're being ridiculous. It was just a blip and meant nothing. I wasn't thinking…"

She stopped talking. His gaze lingered with that dark look she knew well. It was just who he was. She never knew when he'd call her out, but she didn't think he'd let this slide.

"Okay, the truth?" she said. "I wanted anonymity, to do this myself and not have it get back to you or Uncle Marcus or anyone in the family. But, apparently, I can't even do that right. So everyone knows about me. Not sure how I like that."

She thought of Trish, the woman who'd shown her the one-bedroom apartment, and felt another knife in her back.

Her dad didn't say anything for a second. Then he pulled in a breath. "This town knows about all of us. We've been in the spotlight for too long, and it seems everyone knows how to connect the dots between us. Trish wanted a reference. Since you've never rented a place before, it makes people nervous. I vouched for you.

You've got the place if you want it, but why the rush? You're just starting out, just finished high school. You have your own room in a roomy house, and you're just starting to put money away. It's not as if we're at each other's throats."

She didn't know how to explain the feeling that it was time to move out, to move on to her own life. "Dad…seriously, it's time. I just want to have my own place, to be responsible for myself. It has nothing to do with the house being too small. I just want to make decisions for myself, be on my own, pay my own way, walk through the door to something that's just mine. It's not that you'd never see me." She thought of the way her dad poked his nose in her business. At times, she wanted it as much as she didn't. "If you're trying to talk me out of it…"

He lifted his hand and shook his head. "I'm not talking you out of anything. I just wanted to touch base and understand. You know this doesn't mean you get to skip family night." He leaned back in the chair, resting his arm over the back of the empty one beside him. She understood what he was saying, and she didn't know why she wanted to be okay with it.

"I promise I'll be there," she said. The smile burst like a bright beam of sunshine in her stomach and pulled at her face, and her dad gestured to her.

"That there is something I want to see more of, that smile. And one more thing." He leaned across the table, looking to the side, and she held her breath a second, wondering what was coming next. "If your boss touches you like that again, that good ol' boy pat on the back, you tell him to keep his hands to himself, because if he doesn't, it'll be me who's in his face. Use your words and set your boundaries, or I will."

She didn't know what to say. Her dad was serious.

Every time Chad did that, she tried to tell herself that it was normal and shouldn't bother her like it did.

"Okay," she finally said.

He frowned. "Okay what? You'll speak up, or you want me to have a word with him? Because I will. You want me to fight your battles or teach you to fight?"

The answer was on the tip of her tongue as she dragged her gaze over to her boss, who strode out of the back with an apron around his waist, carrying three plates to a table. She knew how he looked at her and everyone else. Her boss was just one more asshole whose name was on her list.

"I'll tell him," she said. "But when he fires me, I'll tell him it was your idea."

Her dad laughed and shook his head. "Ah, Alison, Alison… That's my girl, jumping to the worst-case scenario. But, just FYI, he won't fire you. He can't, because if he does, it won't just be me he'll have to contend with— it'll be all the O'Connells, and I think you know well, darling daughter, that we look after our own. And one other thing: Just remember, when you move out, you can always move back home."

CHAPTER

Two

"I just need your parents to sign an agreement that if you can't pay your rent, they will be responsible, including any damages you may cause."

Alison ground her teeth and bit back the urge to swear under her breath as she squeezed her cell phone. Just down the road was the Bluebird, with customers coming out. Alison wore a black down coat with a faux lined hood, her black jeans, and the old lady black flats that didn't hurt her feet.

"But it's my apartment. Why would you need my parents to sign? That's ridiculous. I have a job…"

"And you're only eighteen, Alison," Trish said. "You have no credit history, so we need someone to vouch for you. It's just how things are done to protect us. Once you have some history behind you, as you pay your rent and look after the place, you won't need a co-signer. At the same time, if this is a problem, there are others we can rent to. There's always a long list…"

"Fine, I get it," she said, cutting in, sensing the woman would go on and on about how irresponsible she expected her to be. "My parents will gladly sign. So how soon until I can get the keys?"

"After you pay the deposit and your first month's rent, and after your parents sign the agreement. There's an addendum you'll have to sign about no smoking and no parties. We'll need cash upfront for the deposit and first month, and then you can have the keys."

For a moment, she wondered what else she'd have to agree to just to have her own place. "I can pay everything today, and I'll ask my dad to call you and stop in today. I'll come back after work." She let it hang, wanting everything yesterday.

"Great! I look forward to hearing from Ryan," Trish said, then hung up.

Alison sent a quick text off to her dad: *Apartment lady needs you to sign your life away in case I screw up. Can you call her please?*

It took only a second before she saw three dots. Her dad was texting something. Then the winking emoji appeared. Her dad was such a dork sometimes—but at the same time, she'd never seen her mom as happy as she'd been since getting back together with him.

She pocketed her phone, unable to keep the smile from her face as she went to pull open the door to the restaurant. At the same time, someone else reached for it. He was tall, with cropped dark hair and dimples.

"Hey there, pretty lady. After you," he said, pulling the door open.

She felt her smile widen, taking in the charm that seemed to flash from the tall, dark, and handsome man. He wore a light gray wool dress coat.

"Well, thank you," she replied. As she stepped inside the restaurant, the sound of cars passing over the slushy streets faded. This early December day was unusually warm. She'd just been there a few hours earlier with her dad for breakfast, and she spotted Nan and Chad running dishes to the back. Half the tables were filled with diners for the lunch rush.

"Alison, I'll get you to start rolling utensils and polishing the glasses in back," Chad tossed out over his shoulder as he strode past the bar. "The dishwasher called in sick, so I need you to pitch in there, as well."

The hot guy was taking off his coat and sliding it over the back of a chair at the bar, which was empty. She hesitated a moment before heading into the back and clocking in, then putting her stuff away in the cubicle where all the employees hung their coats and tossed their bags. She took in Vern, the chef, and Dax, who did everything else.

"Hey there, Alison," Dax said. He had a heavy reddish beard and was an easy forty pounds overweight, with a dirty apron over his large belly. "Didn't know you were working the lunch shift."

"Chad put me back on lunch this week. Said you were short staffed." She made a face.

Vern, who was frying something, glanced her way. She never could figure out what he was thinking. He towered over Dax. "Yeah, heard him redoing the schedule this morning. Seems the new guy lasted only three shifts before giving his notice."

"Alison, for the love of God, get out here and stop dawdling," Chad snapped as he stepped into the back. The door was still open, and the two other men fell quiet. She could see the way Chad looked at her and was sure he didn't talk to anyone else the way he did to her. She felt the reprimand like a slap.

"I just got here," she said. "You said you wanted the glasses polished and utensils rolled." She gestured to the dish pit.

He only shook his head. "Well, it will have to wait. I need you out here now to get drinks and be the bus girl."

Bus girl! She'd really been demoted. That was the job she'd started out with in her first days with the Bluebird, being everyone's slave and getting no tips. She held her tongue.

Chad walked over to the line and tacked an order up for Vern. "I need you to take a ginger ale and one tea to table four with two glasses of water."

"Okay," was all she said, and she didn't miss the look Vern passed her before she walked out of the back.

She took in the handsome man sitting at the bar, alone, as she reached for two glasses and filled them with water. He was wearing a light blue knit sweater. Handsome was an understatement.

"Have you been looked after yet?" she asked.

"Not yet," he replied. "Seems I'm waiting for you."

She hesitated a second, because it seemed like he was flirting…but that was impossible. No one flirted with her. She lifted another glass for the soda. The way he was looking at her, the edge to his smile, he was teasing her—or maybe he wasn't. He leaned back and crossed his arms. Even his chest was impressive.

"What can I get you to drink?" she said as she filled a glass with ginger ale and set it on the tray with the waters, then reached for a mug and small metal pot for the tea.

"Just a coffee, actually, and water and a menu."

She reached for one of the laminate menus stacked behind the bar and rested it on the counter beside him, then set a mug and saucer before him and lifted the coffee carafe to pour.

"Cream and sugar?" she asked. She filled another glass with water and rested it beside the coffee.

He just shook his head as he reached for the mug. "No, no, black is fine."

As she turned back to the tray, Chad appeared behind her. "Hey, I told you to get those drinks over to table four! What's taking you so long?" He settled his hand on her back, that spot between her shoulder blades. She could feel the reprimand from him along with the reminder from her dad.

"I have them ready now," she said, "and please don't touch my back again."

He pulled his hand away, and at the expression on his face, she feared what he'd say. But he just angled his head, took a step back, and held his hands up. "Wasn't sure you were hearing me. I was just trying to get your attention. There was nothing inappropriate there, Alison. You do have a tendency not to hear. If you have the drinks, then get going," he said rather sharply and pointed to the table.

She lifted the tray. As he walked away in back, her tension spiked.

"That was bullshit, you know."

She turned to mister good looking, who was gazing right at her. His hazy blue eyes against mocha skin seemed to add an edge to just how attractive he was.

She just stared at him for a second. "Excuse me?" was all she could think to say.

He leaned on the counter and gestured with his mug of coffee behind her. "Your boss, I take it? Yeah, that wasn't cool, touching you that way, and his explanation was bullshit, the way he flipped the blame when you called him out. Good for you for speaking up. At the same time, I didn't hear an apology from him. Don't let him get away with that," he said. With the strength that seemed to radiate off him, she felt as if she wasn't totally alone.

She glanced over to the door and then back to the

super hot guy. There seemed to be chemistry between them. "Ah, thanks, but when I get fired, being right isn't going to pay my rent."

He laughed as she strode away with the tray over to table four and delivered the drinks. When she glanced back, he was talking to Nan, who was taking his order.

Chad was still in the back. Maybe her dad was right. Everyone seemed to think she had no boundaries, but for the first time, speaking up, she felt as if she'd put Chad Hargrave on notice, and it felt pretty damn good.

As the rest of the lunch shift passed, she rolled the pile of cutlery. By the time she was finished, she glanced up and took in the now virtually empty restaurant. It was close to four thirty. She felt the vibration of her phone in her back pocket and pulled it out, seeing her dad's text: *Signed the required X. You're good to go. See you tonight at Marcus's. Don't be late.*

"Are you suddenly on a break?" Chad snapped as he strode past her. His gaze and reprimand hit their mark.

"Sorry," she said, shoving her phone in her back pocket. "I'm done here with the cutlery. Anything else you want me to do?"

Chad lingered, the distance and tension between them apparent. "Wipe the tables down, and the two booths need cleared. Then I guess you're done for the day."

As he walked away into the back, Nan strode out, carrying a tray filled with dirty glasses. She raised a brow and took in the swinging door behind her before dragging her gaze back to Alison.

"Well, haven't seen Chad that off in a while." She stopped right beside her. "You did good today and held your tongue, considering you were suddenly demoted to bus girl instead of waitress." She rested the tray on the counter of the bar and reached into the pocket of her short black apron to pull out several bills. "Here's some tip money, which you were denied. Thanks for helping. I've told Chad many times to keep his hands to himself. You were right to say something, but next time, do it in private and not in front of the customers. That's why he's so pissed. You embarrassed him."

So she'd heard.

The front door to the restaurant opened, and she spotted Belinda Lee dressed in a long black skirt and red winter jacket, which she unzipped. Her blond hair was pulled back in a tight bun, and her face was the kind of perfection that had Alison wanting to punch her. She smiled brightly, and Alison wondered if she snarled, as she felt Nan's hand on her arm.

"Hi, Belinda, you ready for your first day?" Nan said with that friendly tone of hers.

Belinda stopped at the bar and dragged her gaze over to Alison, then shrugged happily. "Can't wait. Although I've never been a waitress before, Chad assured me I'll have no trouble catching on. Hey, Alison, how are you? Are you working tonight, too?"

Why did she have to be so damn friendly? But then, she'd always been like that—to her face, right before planting a knife in her back.

"No," she replied. She could have said more, but the last thing she wanted was to have any conversation with the girl who'd lied about her in a way that could've ended with her facing charges that would've ruined her life. The gossip had never gone away. Tension lingered.

"Well, Belinda, Chad is in back," Nan said. "You should check in, and he'll walk you through what you need to do."

Belinda dragged her gaze back to her, firmed her lips, and then walked through the back door.

Nan was standing right beside her now, so close, resting her arm on the counter of the dark wood bar. "You want me to say it?" she said, and Alison wondered whether she was in for another scolding.

"What, that I've worked here for a year to land that evening waitress job only to have it ripped away and be reduced to a bus girl, while Belinda walks in with no experience at all, bats her lashes at Chad, and gets the premium shift? Like, what gives?" she said. The anger she'd kept at bay was suddenly simmering to a slow boil.

Nan let out a sigh, one she knew well. "Word of advice: Let it go. I told him not to do it, but he says he sees something in her. I've been working a lot of years, and I haven't always been this happy. There are a lot of Chads out there, but there are also a lot of bosses who are way worse, and I've worked for all of them. I've been passed over for a lot of opportunities I should've had, and I was angry for a long time because of that. Your anger over today is justified, but at the same time, the only person you're hurting is yourself. Do your best, Alison. What you give out is what you get back. I told you before that if you want to be happy and have people treat you fairly, decently, then you need to do the same."

She wondered if it was the expression on her face and the way she pulled back that made Nan angle her head and raise a brow.

"Don't be angry at me," Nan said. "This was my gift to you today. And another thing: There are a lot of Belindas out there, waiting to shove a knife in your back. They seem to be born with the gift of wrapping a man around their finger, but one day..." That was all she said before she lifted the tray.

The door opened to the back, and she heard Chad and Belinda's laughter.

Nan shook her head. "Focus on you, Alison. Take a deep breath. See you tomorrow."

As she strode into the back, past the swinging door, Alison just stared, considering what the older waitress, her mentor, had said. How did she make it seem so easy, as if nothing ever got to her?

Her phone dinged again, and she took in the time on the clock behind the bar. She thought of the keys she'd be holding shortly. Soon, she would have something that was just hers. Maybe Nan was right. Focusing on herself really did make her feel better.

"Well, hello again."

Alison was zipping her purse, having just pulled cash from the ATM, and she turned to take in the hot guy from the restaurant. He was wearing a gray wool coat, dressy, classy, and was walking right toward her.

"Hey there," was all she managed to get out as she took in his smile—for her? She fought the urge to look over her shoulder, expecting him to be talking to someone else, but he stopped right in front of her.

"Alison, right?"

"Yeah, that's right. How did you…?" she started, taking in his dimples as his smile flashed. The man sure had a way of giving everything when he looked at her. She tried to figure out how old he was. Mid-twenties, she thought.

"One of my talents is remembering faces and names. I'm Bennett Warren." He held out his large hand, and she took it, reminding herself of civility. He had remembered her name. That was something that rarely happened.

"Alison O'Connell, your friendly scut worker and restaurant bus girl," she replied. This time, she dropped Sweetgrass, because she remembered her dad's face.

She thought he chuckled, and she wasn't sure what to make of his expression as she shook his hand, not something she did often.

He shrugged. "So you're not only a pretty girl with a pretty name, but you've got a great sense of humor, too. Just getting off work, bus girl?"

She was aware of the fact that her mom was waiting in her Jeep in a parking spot two cars down. "Yeah, done for today." She couldn't remember ever having smiled so easily.

"And your boss is behaving himself? Did he apologize after that dickhead move?"

Holy crap! The guy had remembered that, too. Remembering little things about her was something no one ever did—except Brady, before things became awkward and went sideways. Right, she had to get him out of her head, to move on from that feeling that had her slipping away to the corners on family nights.

"No apologies, but he kept his distance," she said. "Still, I'm sure something will be coming down the pike, retribution of some kind." She could see her mom looking her way now, and she had to pull her gaze back to Bennett, who was still standing there.

"Hey, I get it, but things don't change if you don't speak up, and it's impossible to get anywhere if there's no respect from your manager. At the same time, toxic environments are just that. Hold your head up. Don't take any crap. Your boss is a dick, but you have a great smile. See you around, Alison," he said, then walked around her, into the bank. She found herself turning to watch him, her heart thudding, and she forced herself to pull it together as she walked over to her mom's Jeep, pulled open the passenger door, and slid in.

"Who was that?"

She pulled at her seatbelt and latched it, pulling in a breath before looking over to her mom, who was smiling in a way that had her rolling her eyes. "Just a customer at the restaurant today. He remembered me, is all, and wanted to say hi."

And he was like a knight in shining armor—but she'd keep that part to herself.

"He's cute, and the way he was looking at you… Did he ask you out?" her mom said, darting a gaze back out. Bennett had walked back out and was walking past them, and he looked right at her and smiled, dimples flashing. He lifted his hand in a wave, and it was awkward, especially with her mom. She waved back.

"No, of course not," she said. "He's just a nice guy."

"Mm-hmm," was all her mom said as she started her Jeep.

Alison found herself looking to see where he'd gone, but she didn't see him anymore as they backed out.

"So your dad signed everything for you," her mom said. "I still can't believe you want to move out! It's not too late, you know. You haven't signed the lease yet or paid any money down."

She knew what her mom was doing. At the same time, she couldn't remember the last time she'd been so excited over anything. The appeal of having her own place, independence, and freedom, so to speak, being in charge of just herself, was something she couldn't have explained to anyone.

"Mom, I'm moving out, so if we could just drive to the Carlyle, I'll pay the money and get my keys. I mean, it's time, and this is something I really want."

Her mom lifted a hand from the steering wheel as if to stop her from going on. She signaled her turn around the block, and Alison could see her new home just ahead. It was perfect, only about three blocks from work. She could walk easily and would think about getting a car down the road. Most of all, she wouldn't have her mom and dad there to walk in on her anytime they wanted.

"Fine," Jenny said. "I'm just saying, I don't want to see you move out, but if this is what you want…"

"It is, Mom." She knew she was trying to change her mind. "And, as Dad pointed out this morning when he forced me to go to breakfast with him, I'm still expected at every family night. The only difference is that I'll be sleeping somewhere else. Besides, I want to stand on my own two feet. I have a job. It's not as if I'm leaving the country. Now you and Dad can have time alone. You may even realize how great it is, not having me there," she added as her mom pulled into a spot and put the Jeep in park.

She slid her gaze over to her, and Alison didn't miss the frown. "There you go again, Alison, saying we're better off without you. You know we love you, and I hate to see you running out the door and hurrying to move away just when you and your dad are building something. He loves you, you know. And you're not underfoot."

What the hell was she supposed to say to that? Talking about her feelings was something she didn't do.

"Geez, Mom, seriously, this isn't about you two. It's about me. I'm doing this for me." She fisted her hands, feeling how different things were with her mom after what they'd gone through. She'd never seen her so happy, though, and maybe she wanted the same for herself.

"Alison, don't you think your dad and I have been

worried about you? We've given you space, a lot of space. We know that what happened with Brady crushed you…"

"Mom, stop, already. It's over. I'm over it." She wanted to snarl before her mom poked anymore at a wound that had barely healed.

"No, Alison. I'm not trying to pick a fight here, but you say you're over it even though I know you're not. We all know what it did to you. I saw the light in your eyes, the light you'd managed to get back only for a short time, dim. I know what Wren did, too, and I'm responsible for that. No one deserves that. Since Brady and Cassie eloped a few weeks ago, your dad and I have seen the trouble you're having with her. Can I blame you? No, but she's a nice girl, and you have to find a way—"

"I know, Mom!" she yelled, her hand on the door. She gave it a yank, and it popped open. "Maybe this is one of the reasons I want my own place, so I don't have to have this thing with Brady shoved in my face every time I turn around. I know you're watching me, worrying I'm going to screw up or say or do something wrong, and you all stand back and say, 'Oh, there she goes again, self-sabotaging.' Or maybe you think I'll just fall apart. But I'm not going to fall apart! I'm fine, and if it's all the same to you, I'd rather just forget about it and not talk about it, because what hurts is the fact that you keep bringing it up. Do me a favor and stop. Stop talking about it. Stop worrying I'm going to break, because I'm not. I'm stronger than that, Mom. You and Wren made sure of that. Stop expecting the worst of me."

Then she stepped out of her mom's Jeep and closed the door, feeling like shit for tossing Wren in her mom's face. She heard her mom step out, as well, and when she looked over to her, she saw her hands lifted in surrender— but she also saw the shadow of hurt.

Four

"Man, this is so cute! You scored big here," Suzanne said. She was wearing a red hat with white stripes and a pompom as she leaned against the counter beside Alison.

Alison could hear her uncles lugging up what she thought was an old sofa that had belonged to Suzanne, and she opened a box of dishes labeled *Karen*, taking in the dated old carpet that had been freshly steam cleaned, the door to the open bedroom, and the bathroom across from it. The kitchen, although dated too, was open to the living room, and seeing it now, she was counting the minutes until everyone was gone and she could bask in something that was just hers.

"So tell me, is there a hot guy that goes with this place?" Suzanne asked.

Alison watched her dad and Owen struggle in with a lot of grunting before flipping over the orange sofa and setting it down in the small living room.

"No hot guy, sorry, but you're right that it's nice, and I can't tell you how frickin' awesome this is, having my own place. And, in case I didn't say it, thanks for all the stuff. I didn't expect you all to furnish it and supply me with dishes, too. I don't think I'll have to buy anything."

Suzanne only shrugged. "You have any idea how great this is for us? We can finally get rid of so much we've been hanging on to. That's the great thing about you and Brady: We can pass on all the old things we haven't figured out how to get rid of."

Alison opened the box and saw the pretty flowered dishes.

Suzanne's hand slid over hers. "Karen wanted you to have those. She knows how much you loved them. The towels are from your grandma, too. By the way, I talked to her this morning. She's going to call you later. I think she misses you, and Eva and Cameron, too, more than any of us."

"Hey, you two! There're still more boxes downstairs to bring up," Ryan said, walking over. As he ruffled her hair, she thought she heard Marcus swearing outside somewhere on the stairs. "Marcus and Harold are bringing up the bed. I don't think you'll hear the end of it, renting a third-floor apartment with no elevators."

She didn't miss the smile Suzanne tried to hide. Alison knew she would fall into bed tonight from all the exercise she hadn't planned on having.

"Sorry, but I appreciate the help just the same," she said.

Her dad's gaze lingered for a second as he looked around at the dark brown cupboards, saying nothing. She felt a tap on her arm from Suzanne.

"You know what? Why don't we go get refreshments for everyone?" her aunt said, maybe to save her from having to listen to her dad telling her again that he didn't want her to move out, that she could come home anytime, or something along those lines that could suddenly turn the moment awkward.

"Jenny is picking up some groceries," he added. "She and Charlotte wanted to surprise you."

She felt the pull on her arm from Suzanne, who said, "Then we'll pick up some beer," before pulling her along.

Just then, there was a tap on the open door, and there was Cassie, holding a plant, her dark hair a curly mess, and Brady behind her, all smiles, carrying a box.

"Hey there! Wow, this is so nice," Cassie said as she stepped in.

Brady walked past his wife and said, "Where do you want the boxes?"

Alison gestured to the wall. "Anywhere is fine," she said.

Cassie kept walking toward her, holding out the plant. "This is from me and Brady, a little housewarming gift. It's just a plant, but we wanted to get you something."

For a second, she stood there, knowing she needed to say thank you. She felt a nudge from Suzanne, who reached for the plant for her.

"Yeah, thanks, that's really nice," was all she could get out. "We're just going to make a beer run for everyone. Sodas?"

Cassie shrugged. "Sure, whatever you pick up would be great. Can I give you a hand unpacking anything while you're gone?"

She was so nice, and Alison felt like absolute shit for letting the awkwardness linger. She felt a nudge again from her aunt.

"Sure. The boxes on the counter are dishes and stuff. If you want to unpack some, that would be great."

Then Marcus and Harold made their way in, both in

winter bomber jackets, carrying her mattress. She didn't miss the pointed look.

"You're going to owe us big time for this, kid," Marcus said. "Third floor, all stairs, and we still have your dresser, the table and chairs from Karen, and how many more boxes?"

She knew he was all bark, but she said, "You know I'll pay up. Free babysitting, my time, my blood… Thanks for hauling everything up. We'll pick up the beer for you."

Suzanne said something to Harold, and he put his end of the bed down and pulled his wallet from his pocket.

"Great, but don't be long," Marcus said. "Brady, we could use you downstairs to bring up the chairs. You can help Ryan and Owen with the table."

Suzanne had her moving out the open door, and she could hear the voices behind her as they hurried down the stairs, Suzanne shoving money from Harold into her jacket pocket. Behind were her dad and Brady, and ahead were Owen and Tessa at the truck, reaching for a box.

"Hey, where are you two slipping off to?" Tessa called, wearing a white hat with a pompom and a dark blue winter coat. Her blond hair was long and tied back.

"Beer and food," Suzanne called out. "We expect everything unloaded by the time we get back!"

She maneuvered Alison toward Harold's new Kia, where Alison slid in the passenger side, and Suzanne started the car and backed out. She couldn't shake the feeling that Suzanne had something on her mind.

"You really think they'll have everything unloaded by then?"

Suzanne pulled out of the parking lot. "Oh, I guarantee it—but I wanted to have a talk with you without everyone listening in. You know Ryan is worried about you, and Jenny is still reeling a bit over the other day. She told me about what you said, how you blame her about Wren. I have to tell you, kiddo, that wasn't cool. Your mom was really hurt."

She knew she'd hurt her mom. That was something she'd seen Wren do time and again, too: the words, the cutting remarks, the slaps. Her mom had just taken it. There were times Alison thought she was too much like a man she wasn't even related to.

"I didn't mean to hurt her, but she's constantly coming at me. I just said it."

Alison had learned to swallow a lot before snapping, lashing out with words she wished she could take back. She was strong, with a thick skin that was pretty beaten up, but she was tired of being seen as a freak.

"No one's coming at you, Alison. Ryan and Jenny, just like all of us, want to see you happy. We're in your corner, so how about not tossing out any more remarks about Wren? Your mom, everything she's done is for you. I heard only some of the things that happened, but I'm sure there's more. I can tell you from experience that parents aren't perfect, but family is family. We've all screwed up, you included, and me too, but we don't go around using the ones we love as a punching bag."

Alison took in the supermarket, Donnelly's, as they pulled in, seeing the beer and wine store next door. "I get it," she said. "Consider me reprimanded. I'll apologize to my mom. Is there anything else?"

Suzanne turned off the vehicle and reached over. "Yeah. Try harder with Cassie. I think if you let yourself get past all that hurt and anger—and no one is saying you're not justified in feeling that way—you'll see that Cassie isn't the bad guy. We've all had shit tossed at us. Going around being angry is allowed for a bit, but not forever." She leaned on her door and gave Alison a look, followed by a smile only Suzanne could toss out.

"So is this when I need to start inviting her over for tea?" Alison said.

Suzanne made a face. "No, but it wouldn't hurt for you to try to get to know her. She's family now." She stepped out of the vehicle, and Alison did too. "I'll get the beer. You go and pick out some sodas." She reached into her pocket and pulled out some bills, then handed her twenty dollars. "From Harold's stash," she said, holding it out.

Alison took the money. "You ever feel like a kept woman, Suzanne?"

Her aunt's eyes sparkled with mischief, and her lips twitched in amusement. "All the time, but it works." She shrugged. "Didn't say I was perfect."

As Suzanne walked off and pulled open the door of the beer and wine shop, Alison wondered about her quirky aunt, who seemed to be settling into living with Harold, not working. Maybe someone needed to give her some advice, some action items she could address to fix her life, find a job, and get past the fact that she was no longer a firefighter and never would be again.

Alison started over to Donnelly's Market.

"Hey, Alison, is that you?"

She turned and saw Bennett, flashing that same charming smile, in the same wool coat but with dark jeans now, walking her way.

"Bennett, what are you doing here?"

He stopped right in front of her. "Just got off a two-day shift and thought of picking up some groceries. So how's your boss treating you? Need me to stop on by and add some muscle?"

The way he said it with a smile, she couldn't stop the laugh that seemed to come from nowhere. "No need to step in yet, but I'll let you know. He's pretty much demoted me, but hey, it could be worse. He could've fired me. So, a two-day shift. What do you do?"

She wondered how tall he was. Her dad's height, she thought, with a nice build. There was something about the way he held himself. Looking at him, she realized she hadn't felt this good in a long time.

"I'm a med student. Just got away from the hospital. You're in good company with the scut work. I'm the helper and do all the shit jobs, so I commiserate and understand completely. But yes, being employed is a very good thing. You're absolutely right."

"Wow, I'm impressed. A med student…so you're studying to be a doctor?"

He just shrugged. There was something about the way he was looking at her, as if he really wanted to talk to her. "Yeah, well, med student is a long way from doctor, a lot of years as a bottom-feeder, working my way up."

Then he said nothing and just smiled at her. Neither moved for a second. There was tension and chemistry. He pulled in a breath and glanced past her. "Well, I guess I should get some groceries before I fall over from exhaustion. It was great to see you again, Alison. Maybe I'll drop in to your restaurant again soon."

He started walking, but then he turned back to her, still stepping backwards. "And the offer stands: If you need some muscle or just a friendly face to show up and let your boss know that he can't treat you like shit, then I'm ready, willing, and happy to oblige."

She just lifted her hand. "Thanks, Bennett. When you stop by the restaurant, your coffee's on me."

He gestured to her, and something about his smile warmed her in ways no one's ever had before. "It's a date,

Alison O'Connell," he called out, then lifted his hand and turned to walk to the grocery store.

"Who was that?" Suzanne whispered beside her.

Alison jumped as she took in her aunt, who was right there, looking dorky in that red and white hat, holding a case of beer, staring at Bennett as he walked away.

"Just someone I met at work, a customer, a nice guy. He's a med student."

Suzanne raised a brow and dragged her gaze over to where Bennett was now walking into the grocery store. "He said the word 'date,' and I can see by the way you're watching him that you like him."

Alison pressed her lips together but couldn't keep from smiling as she shook her head. Then she started laughing.

Suzanne gasped. "Oh, you really do like him! I was so kidding about the hot guy, but now I see you've been holding out. Is he single? Come on, he's cute. Tell me everything. You've been holding out on me, my sweet little niece."

Alison just shook her head. "No, I just met him a few days ago, but you know what? You're right. I like him. I have no idea if he's single, but he sees me, he talks to me. Anyway, I'm going to go in and get the soda. I'm not talking about this anymore with you."

"Get his number if you see him in the store," Suzanne called out as Alison started walking.

She just shook her head. There was something about seeing Bennett Warren again. Things really were looking up. She had her very first place, her own apartment that was all hers, and then there was this guy she kept running into, as if fate was conspiring in a good way.

Bennett distracted her. He didn't see her the same way other people did, as if she were wearing a "Kick me" sign, as if she would never really fit in.

It was cold, and it was already close to dark as she approached her building, seeing the stairwell outside and her living room window, which faced the courtyard. The lamp in the living room was on, since there was just something about walking into a darkened house that had always bothered her, though she'd been unwilling to admit to herself that she was scared.

"Alison, is that you?"

She turned and took in the white Volvo, then realized it was Bennett stepping out. He closed the door and locked it, wearing a dark bomber jacket, and he ran his hand over his short dark hair as he walked over to her.

"Hi, what are you doing here?" she said.

"I live here," he replied, gesturing at the building.

In that moment, it seemed the stars had suddenly aligned. As he strode up beside her, she admired the way he walked, the way he carried himself, and the way he smiled down at her again.

"Here at the Carlyle?" she said. Boy, she sounded like an idiot, and for a second she wished she could take it back. Maybe that was why his expression suddenly seemed filled with amusement. She thought he wanted to laugh.

"Yes, here at the Carlyle. Are you visiting someone?"

She shoved her hands in her pockets and then pulled them out. "No, I just moved in yesterday. So we're neighbors, then?" she said, feeling the smile pulling at her lips.

His gaze… She couldn't remember the last time a man had given her everything the way he was—not since Brady. Yet here she was, feeling as if everything was almost perfect.

"It appears so," he said, then added teasingly. "I guess if I run out of sugar, I can knock on your door."

She turned with him and took a step, walking side by side. She wondered where he lived. "Anytime. I'm up on the third floor." She gestured up. "That's my apartment there, with the light on."

He had his hands in his pockets, and the way he looked over to her, that smile, seemed so genuine and warm. "Well, this really is a small world. Seems fate is aligning for us. Looks like I actually am your neighbor. Was wondering who had moved in there. Guess you'll be really close when I need to borrow that cup of sugar."

He gestured for her to go first up the stairs, and she started up, feeling him walking behind her. Maybe this was the time to ask if there was a missus or someone he was unofficially involved with, but she didn't want to. With how suddenly quiet he was, he seemed distracted, and she couldn't think of what else to say, considering small talk had never been her thing.

"Goodnight, Bennett," she finally said as she pulled her keys from her pocket and stopped at her door.

He hesitated a second as he started to the neighboring door, then stepped back to her, pulling in a breath. She could see an edge tonight that she hadn't seen in him before. He glanced to her door and then lowered his gaze to her.

"You know, I had an absolutely shitty day today, and all I wanted to do when I left the hospital was go home and forget, or try to. I was going to order a pizza and grab a beer, but now I'm thinking that staring at four walls alone after the day I've had is exactly what I don't want. You want to grab a bite to eat, or maybe we could order something in? Unless you have plans."

He let it linger, and it took her brain a moment to realize he was kind of asking her out, Bennett Warren, this good-looking guy she'd just met, who wasn't looking at her as if she were some misfit.

"No plans for me," she said. "Yeah, we could order something, or I could put some pasta on. Was planning on spaghetti tonight. You could come in, and I'll cook…" She slid her key in her lock as he nodded and gestured to his door.

"Better your place than mine," he said. "I haven't picked up in a while, so mine is actually quite the disgusting mess. Spaghetti sounds perfect."

She unlocked her door and stepped inside, seeing the orange sofa and coffee table, the small flatscreen TV, and the table in the dining area. Everything had come from someone in her family, a hand-me-down, and in that second, as she saw it all, she really did feel wanted.

Bennett stepped in behind her and closed the door as she shrugged out of her coat and pulled open the closet door. She reached for an empty hanger, feeling her heartbeat kick up as he took his coat off too. She handed him a hanger and took in the way he glanced around at her apartment.

"Wow, this is nice. You just moved in? Looks like you have nothing left to unpack."

She walked into her kitchen, to the small island. She needed a second to settle her thoughts and pull it together. What was it about this guy? She realized Bennett really was interested in her. The attraction simmered, and she didn't think it was one sided.

"Well, my family helped—my parents, my aunts and uncles. They made it relatively easy. It felt like everyone was here, unpacking and putting everything away, even though I wouldn't have minded doing it myself. I have to pinch myself to remember this is mine, all mine. It's kind of nice coming home to find everything done. I can't believe you live right next door. This is, like, so cool."

He went right to a photo of her family, her mom and dad on the day they were married. It had been a happy day, for a moment, until the rug had been yanked out right from under her. She wasn't sure what to make of the way he was looking at it, as he said nothing.

"My mom and dad got married last year—well, a little over a year ago. That's us in the photo."

She pulled a pot out from beside the stove, a white older stove with coil burners, and filled it with water to boil, then opened the well-stocked cupboard, courtesy of her mom and Charlotte. All her favorites were there. She really did need to thank them, and she needed to tell her mom she was sorry for being such a bitch at times.

She reached for the jar of spaghetti sauce and pulled it out, then remembered the ground beef in the fridge.

"So your mom and dad were never married?" he said.

She had her back to Bennett as she pulled out a frypan, then opened the fridge and pulled out the beef. She turned to him. "No. It's kind of a long story, actually. I grew up thinking another man was my father, but then I found out from him, during one of his drunken asshole moments, that he wasn't. Anyway, we moved here, right next door to

Ryan O'Connell, who turned out to be my biological father. Now my mom and Ryan are married and together, and I have an instant family I never had before—uncles, aunts, a grandmother…"

And a grandfather, but she couldn't talk about that, and she wondered if she'd ever really know Raymond O'Connell.

"You want ground beef in your sauce," she said, "or do you prefer meatless?"

He put the photo back on the table beside the sofa, exactly where her mom had set it up. "Yes to the ground beef. So what about your other father, the man who raised you? Do you still see him?"

She had her back to Bennett again as she dumped the meat in the frypan, and she hesitated a second as she thought of Wren Sweetgrass, a man who had doted on her. As she thought back now to him and the cruel, cutting remarks he'd made to her mom, she wondered if that was why she struggled, always self-sabotaging her happiness.

Then Bennett was right beside her as she reached for a wooden spoon from the utensil drawer. He took it from her and started breaking up the ground beef as if making himself at home. "I hope I didn't ask something I shouldn't have," he said. "Just by your face, I see I hit a nerve."

She pulled in a breath. "Sorry, it was just a rough time. He died. Actually, he was killed. That was why we moved here. I haven't really thought about that in a while. My life went from dark and twisty, even though I didn't realize it at the time, to something brighter, with an instant family. My father now is the opposite of Wren…"

He glanced over his shoulder to her, and she wasn't sure what to make of the expression.

She felt awkward as she shrugged. "That was his name, Wren Sweetgrass. He was a complicated man. Ryan, my real dad, would never do the kinds of things Wren did. I don't even know how to explain it, but it was almost normal for me, the way I grew up, so it makes real normality a struggle to handle. So how about you? Tell me about your family."

He worked the ground beef, breaking it up into small pieces. For a moment, she wasn't sure he'd answer, and she could feel the silence slipping into awkwardness. Then he tapped the wooden spoon on the side of the frypan, pulled in a breath, and turned to face her.

"I guess family is complicated. I wonder if normal really exists. Not in my world, it sure didn't. My mother is dead, but it was just her and me when I was growing up. I became a doctor because of her. My father...I had met him only a few times. After my mother died, I went looking for him."

He said nothing else, but there was just something about the way he was talking. The smiling, happy, warm, and charismatic Bennett had been replaced with this guy who seemed deep in thought, and she didn't sense anything happy.

"Did you find him?" she said.

He turned back to the stove as if thinking, then dragged his gaze back to her. No smile, nothing. He made a face and shook his head, forcing a tight smile to his lips, one that didn't meet his eyes. "No. That opportunity was taken from me."

She wasn't sure what he was saying. "Taken from you...in what way?"

He shrugged, reaching for the sauce. He opened it and smelled it before pouring it over the ground beef. "He'd been murdered. Guess you and I have that in common, too."

He put the jar down and stirred the sauce, and she just stared at his back. He had said it so matter of factly.

The pot started rattling as the water boiled, and Bennett lifted the lid. Alison pulled open the cupboard and reached for the package of spaghetti, taking in this man. There was something about him that seemed comfortable and familiar—but something complicated, too.

CHAPTER
Six

The sun was shining bright today, and Alison couldn't remember ever having been able to smile with such ease. In fact, she couldn't pull the smile from her face. She even lifted a hand to wave to people she knew as they passed her on the street. For a moment, she wondered who this new Alison was, so much so that she had to fight the urge to laugh.

Feeling this good, she knew, was all because of Bennett. Every step she took, she felt the lightness in her walk. Lifting her head, it was as if she'd missed out on feeling the sun on her face for her entire life. That dark cloud that seemed to linger over her head had suddenly vanished. She'd never felt the kind of joy and excitement for life that she did right now.

Last night, she and Bennett had sat at the old kitchen table with their dirty spaghetti plates still in front of them, talking about everything and nothing. She couldn't remember ever having been able to talk so easily with someone before. Awkwardness just didn't seem to exist with Bennett. She hadn't wanted the night to end, and it had been after midnight when he'd finally said goodnight. For a moment, he had stared at her in the doorway, then leaned down and pressed a brief, gentle kiss to her lips.

It seemed as if she'd known him forever.

Feeling this good, she swore that everything about her life was turning a corner, as if there really was hope. Maybe her family had been right every time they'd said to look on the bright side and keep her chin up, that it wasn't all bad.

Alison crossed the busy street, hearing the slushy snow on the road as she spotted the restaurant. Even knowing she'd had her hours cut and her prime shift taken from her didn't bother her in the least as she pulled on the door. But the door was locked. She yanked it again, hearing the rattle, and then spotted someone inside, coming her way. She cupped her hands on the door and looked in past the glare, seeing Nan and Vern—and her uncle Marcus?

The door was pushed open by Vern, the tall, lanky chef.

"Why is the door locked?" Alison said. "Is something going on?" She stepped past Vern inside.

His expression was grim as he nodded. "Chad's on his way to the hospital. He was found in the storage room, assaulted."

For a moment, she didn't know what to say. She thought of the boss she hated as she listened to the lock of the door behind her. By the expressions on Vern's face, she thought there was more, and that feeling of unease that had been her constant companion returned just like that, as if everyone was against her or would be looking at her as if she'd done something.

"What's going on?" she said as she walked over to Marcus.

He dragged his gaze from where he'd been writing

something on his notepad. Next to him, Nan was wearing her coat. Alison took in the tables and dirty dishes and half-eaten food. From what she could see, people had just up and left.

"Your boss was found in the storage room," Marcus said. "We believe he was struck from behind, attacked. It appears as if someone tried to hide him. Foul play, it looks like. We're talking to everyone."

For a second, she wasn't sure she'd heard right. She looked over to Nan and back to her uncle. "You're not serious. So what did he do to deserve that fate?" was all she could think to say, and she didn't miss the way her uncle's gaze lingered on her as if he couldn't believe she'd said what she did. Was this a big joke?

"This is so awful, Alison," Nan cut in. "We opened as usual, but Chad wasn't here. I can't remember him not showing up before. I asked Vern and Dax, but no one had heard from him. I was going to call his wife, Pam, but then it was busy, and we were almost done the breakfast rush before he was found. How long was he lying back there, unmoving…?" She gestured toward the back room.

Alison had never seen Nan this rattled before.

"You know," she continued, "if Vern hadn't gone in back for the fruit, I don't think we'd have found him."

Marcus turned from Nan and gestured to Alison, who shoved her hands back in her down jacket pockets and started walking with him. His hand was on her back, moving her away from the people she worked with. Through the small window into the kitchen, she spotted Dax talking to Harold.

"Not sure how comfortable I am, having you here, working here, with this going on," Marcus said.

He had her off to the side now, and as she looked around, all she could see was the rent she needed to pay going down the drain. Though there was no love lost between her and Chad, if something happened to him, where would her paycheck come from? She reminded herself she couldn't say that. She was supposed to be concerned about a man who'd never really treated her fairly.

"Is there something you're not telling me, something I should be worried about?" Alison said. "Was this a break-in? You have to know something."

He didn't say anything for a moment. His dark hair was a little longish, just covering the tips of his ears, and she couldn't help wondering when her aunt Charlotte would start nagging him that it was time for a cut. "Do you know anyone who would want to hurt him, your boss?" Marcus said. "Because the way he was found is a little troubling to me."

"You're saying it's not an accident? Maybe he fell," she said, shrugging.

Her uncle glanced away toward Vern and Nan, who were huddled now, talking. Both appeared tense, upset. "No. The medics who were here said he had been hit. He must've been dragged in behind the cases of produce, which were stacked as if someone was trying to hide him. There was a trail from his head wound to show he had been dragged," Marcus said. "I'm troubled about this situation. No word on how long he had been lying there, and we still don't know how he's doing yet. The chef got here first, but I'm still trying to get a timeline together of who was all here and when. Who has access to the back? Then there's his wife, whom I still need to talk to. Alison, you worked for the man, so is there anyone who has a problem with Chad? Any employees with grievances, issues, anything?" The way her uncle said it had her realizing he was serious.

"Well, you mean other than me?" she said. "I had to tell him just yesterday to keep his hands to himself, and he was mighty pissed about that. I kept expecting him to tell me I was through. Dad saw him doing that touchy thing on my back just yesterday and insisted I speak up or he would. You mean that kind of issue?"

She knew she was poking the bear by the way Marcus really looked at her, his expression filled with alarm. She wondered whether he'd walk her out of there so they could have a one-on-one talk with no one else listening.

"I seriously hope you're kidding," he said. "You'd best not joke about that, Alison. This is a serious situation. Even with me, you can't go around saying stuff like that. Did anyone hear you say that to him?"

She realized he was worried, but she just shrugged. "Well, yeah, of course. Nan heard, and there was a…" There was Bennett, but she wasn't ready to have her uncle or family anywhere in his face. No, there was no way he was talking with Bennett. "A customer. But it was no big deal, so you can take that worried expression off your face. He was inappropriate, and I told him so. End of story."

Marcus didn't pull that all-cop gaze from her at first. Then he pulled in a breath and looked past her, over to the door, as if considering something. When he looked back to her, it was with the same eyes as her dad's, that O'Connell blue that could be filled with mischief or burn with the kind of anger and overprotectiveness she'd often experienced.

"You serious about having to tell him to keep his hands off you?" Marcus said. "He was touching you inappropriately?"

She didn't miss the edge to his voice, the anger. She thought he'd likely have a word with Chad, as well, if he recovered. Maybe that was a good thing.

"He likes to put his hands on my back when he's telling me to do something," she said, "like yesterday, when he demoted me from the evening waitress position I worked my ass off for to working only half days as a helper, not even waiting tables."

He looked up and over her head again, still keeping her off to the side, his mouth open as if wanting to say something but unable to find the words. Right, she'd seen that very expression on her dad's face before.

"Okay, let's table the demotion part for now and talk about his wandering hands," Marcus said. He glanced over to Nan and Vern and then looked back at her. "He do that with anyone else here?"

There was something weird about being questioned by her uncle, the sheriff. She knew he didn't let things slide, just like her dad, so she shrugged. "He didn't treat anyone quite like me. He even whistled at me like you would at a dog. Come to think of it, though, sure, he put his hands on everyone except Vern and Dax. It was something he did with women. I've seen him stop and talk with Nan, but I don't remember if his hands have ever been on her. You should ask her. She never seems as if anything bothers her, though. As far as I know, they get along just fine. With Vern and Dax, too, I can't see a problem there. He has a different relationship with them. Then there's Belinda, his new girl and favorite. You should ask her, too."

There was shock and surprise in the way her uncle inclined his head. "We're not talking about Belinda Lee, are we?"

She nodded, for the first time feeling as if she were the one with the answers. "The very same. She walked in here and landed the coveted evening job with no experience except for her flirty smile and knowledge of how to work the situation with a guy. Chad loved her, and next I know,

I'm back working this crap shift, and she's got my job. You say he's been found hit over the head? Yeah, you should go and talk to Belinda."

She knew she was being a little shit, but she wanted her uncle shining a spotlight on Belinda. The girl had lied too many times, made up stories about her, and it seemed she'd gotten only a slap on the wrist. And now, as a reward, she could walk right in and take her job, too.

"I'll be talking to Belinda," Marcus said, "but, Alison, listen to me. I don't want you telling anyone what you said to me about your dad, you understand? I get you and where this is coming from, but someone else would take it the wrong way. You know we've been very much under the spotlight, more than I'm comfortable with, for too long."

There it was, that O'Connell overprotectiveness, a reminder of how things tended to go wrong in their family.

"Of course, I get it," she said.

Her uncle rested his hand on her shoulder and said, "You know what? I'm almost done here, and then I'll take you home."

"You know I have a job here," she started, but Marcus was already shaking his head.

"Not today, you don't. This is a crime scene. No one is staying."

"Marcus," Harold called out. He lifted his hand to Alison and jutted his chin, and she waved back. Her family was the law, and here they were in the restaurant where she worked.

She found herself walking over to Nan and Vern as her uncle wandered over to Harold and Dax. What was up with the two of them?

"My uncle said we have to leave," Alison said. "Any idea who would do this? I mean, did he have any enemies?" She pulled her arms across her chest.

"Kind of creepy, if you ask me," Vern said. "Dax and I were back there, cooking breakfast for how many customers, and there was Chad, unconscious in the back. I mean, if I hadn't sent Dax back for those lemons…"

"I thought you were the one who found him," Nan said, confusion darting across her face.

Vern shook his head and shrugged with an odd, frustrated expression. The way he pulled his hand over his face, she could see how bothered he was. "Nope. I was in the middle of an order and sent Dax back. He was supposed to have everything prepped this morning. He usually does. Actually, this was the first time he didn't. There were no oranges or lemons. The bin was empty."

She glanced over to where Dax was talking with Harold and Marcus, then turned to Nan, who was staring directly at Vern with an odd curiosity.

"So when do you think we'll hear something about our jobs?" Vern said. "I mean, do we come to work tomorrow…?"

The way Nan stared at him, Alison wondered whether she was going to yell at him. "A man is in the hospital and could very well die or never wake up, and you're worried about your job?"

Alison wondered if she made a face, considering Vern had only voiced what she was thinking.

"Of course it's a bad thing," Vern said, "but the world doesn't stop revolving because someone is hurt. I still have to live. I still have to pay bills and keep a roof over my head. I need to know if I need to start looking for another job."

She dragged her gaze from Nan to Vern, then shrugged and nodded in agreement. "Vern's right. The question is do we still have a job, and is the restaurant open or closed tomorrow? And who would do this to Chad?"

Nan pulled in a breath and looked over to her. She seemed to consider something, then lifted her hands. "Well, the only one who can answer that is in the hospital. Consider this: If he wakes up, if he's okay, then I suppose we'll know who did this. If not, I would think we'll hear from his wife about what will happen to the restaurant and when we'll open again. Otherwise, I'm sure he'll be barking orders from his hospital bed, considering Pam has never had any involvement in the restaurant."

Alison remembered meeting Chad's wife only a few times. She didn't really know her, but, on seeing them together, her first impression had been that they just didn't seem to fit. The woman wasn't bad looking. She stood there with her coworkers, saying nothing for a moment.

"Okay, and say he doesn't wake up and the worst-case scenario happens," Alison said. "If it's all the same to you, that seems to be how things work in my life. Then what?"

She wondered whether, by the way Vern looked at her, he was thinking the same thing.

Nan sighed and lifted her hands. "Well, if we don't have a clear idea by tomorrow, that might be a sign that you need to start looking for another job," she said.

There it was, that sinking feeling. That dark cloud, which had been her constant companion, suddenly reappeared.

Marcus had insisted on driving Alison over to his place instead of taking her home to her apartment. Riding in his sheriff's car and walking into his house had her feeling very much as though she were just a kid, living back at home again, being told what to do, suddenly no longer independent and responsible for just herself.

"You don't have to organize my day, you know," she said. "I have things to do."

"I would feel more comfortable with you here right now," Marcus said, "considering I have no idea what went down at that restaurant. Until I do, I want to make sure you're not in the line of fire for any reason. Humor me, please. You know that as soon as I told your dad, he'd have been down there, bringing you back home himself. When bad things happen in this family, things suddenly go south quickly. So again, humor me, okay?"

He strode over to a babbling Cameron in his playpen, and Alison could hear the voices of her mom and Charlotte in the kitchen.

"Hey, you," Marcus said as he leaned down and picked his son up. "Who left you here to entertain yourself?"

Cameron squealed in excitement as Marcus held him in his sheriff's jacket. Alison shrugged off her coat, kicked off her shoes, and started into the kitchen.

"What are you doing here?" Jenny said, giving her a wide smile.

Charlotte angled her head as Marcus strode over, leaned down, and kissed her, Cameron still babbling away in his arms. There was just something about the love Marcus had for his family, for all of them. She had to look away.

"Oh, Uncle Marcus insisted on bringing me here," she said. "The restaurant is closed down today because someone tried to hurt my boss. He was found back in the cold storage, hit over the head."

Jenny glanced at her in alarm. "What? What happened? You're okay? Maybe you shouldn't be working there." She slid her arm around Alison's shoulders.

Charlotte looked up at Marcus as if waiting for more, but Marcus was watching Alison with that expression that was only for her, as if he was about to sigh heavily in exasperation and set her straight. She could predict the buttons she seemed to be able to push with the men in her family.

"We don't know all the details yet," Marcus said. "In fact, we don't know anything, but since foul play is involved, the restaurant isn't opening today. All the other employees have also been sent home, and there's a notice on the door for customers. Harold is still there, handling the investigation, but I need to go back. I need to have a word with Chad's wife, as well. We're still waiting for word from the hospital. So far, he hasn't woken up to tell us who did this."

Her uncle gestured toward her with his free hand

before rubbing Cameron's back, then kissing the top of his head. His expression turned doting every time he looked at his son, but as soon as he glanced back to her, the happy father changed into the sheriff.

"I figured, since Alison has a free day," he continued, "she could help you with my campaign stuff, whatever it is you're organizing to keep me in the job I love. Alison can do her part to make sure my opponent doesn't get the chance to turn this town upside down with his own brand of law."

She knew her uncle was referring to Lonnie, the deputy he had always butted heads with, who was now running against him.

Marcus slid Cameron into her arms just as his cell phone rang, and it wasn't lost on her that everyone saw her as a built-in babysitter. She held Cameron on her hip, and he kicked his legs and held a teething ring in his chubby little fingers, smiling at her with that goofy, drooling grin. He shoved the chunky teething ring in his mouth and chewed. He was really cute, and she loved him, but she still had her heart set on getting back to her own place and not being told what to do. She wondered how long she'd have to stay before she could talk her mom into driving her home.

Her uncle now had his back to them, and she wasn't sure who he was talking to. She only heard him say, "Shit, of all days... Fine. Yeah, I can't believe this. I'll be right there." He turned back as he shoved his cell phone in his pocket. "Seems to be a day of assaults. You remember Hunter, one of the kids involved in Jackson's accidental death at the school? Seems someone tried to run him down."

Alison just stared for a moment as her mom and Charlotte asked, at the same time, "What? That's horrible!" and "Who would do something like that?"

All she could think was that Hunter was just one more person who'd been nasty and mean to her, treating her like she was disposable. She wasn't, though. Maybe there was such a thing as karma, after all. First Chad, now Hunter. For a moment, she wasn't sure how to feel. All she wanted to do was go home and then tell Bennett. Maybe he'd understand why she wasn't totally upset about this.

"Okay, well, I've got to go," Marcus said. "And you..." He turned to Alison, resting his hand on Cameron's head, looking right at her. "Thanks for helping."

All she could do was shrug. "You didn't give me much of a choice."

Her uncle smiled that lopsided smile—as if he'd planned for exactly this scenario, arranging her exactly where he wanted her, tucked away at his place with her mom and his wife while he set out to handle things.

He leaned over and kissed Charlotte, then started out of the kitchen, and she heard the front door. At the same time, she heard Suzanne's voice, and she stepped over to see her aunt coming in as Marcus was going out. Their exchange was brief, and Marcus playfully slugged Suzanne's shoulder. Seeing the teasing between the siblings, she wondered how different she'd be if she'd grown up in this family.

"You know," Charlotte said, "since you're here and not working today, would you mind picking up Eva from school later? I know she misses you."

For a second, she wanted to say no, but Suzanne slipped in, all wide eyed, and headed right over to Alison before she could answer.

"So, tell me," Suzanne said, "did you see mister tall, dark, and extremely attractive again?"

She knew Charlotte and her mom were listening, and she could even feel them lean in, taking in the mischievous grin on Suzanne's face, which always seemed to coincide with the sparkle in those O'Connell blue eyes. Alison said nothing and felt Charlotte poke her back.

"You holding out on us, Alison? Who is this guy?"

Jenny dragged her gaze from Suzanne back to Alison, and she wondered if she could see the smile she knew was tugging at her lips as she held Cameron and swayed back and forth.

"Oh my good God, Alison!" Suzanne jabbed her finger toward her. "You did see him again."

Alison shrugged, knowing her mom was giving her everything.

"Okay, spill, Alison. What's his name?" Charlotte said.

Alison could see her mom was thinking by the way she narrowed her eyes.

"He's not the good-looking guy who was talking to you outside the bank, is he?" Jenny said.

She pulled in a breath and started to shake her head, because the last thing she wanted was her family jumping on Bennett and this new and too-perfect thing she had with him.

"Bennett Warren is his name," Alison said. "Yes, I saw him, okay? Just so you know, none of you are allowed to show up and ruin things, but he lives right next door to me."

Suzanne gasped, and she wasn't sure what to make of the exchange between Charlotte and her mom.

"Well, that's handy," Charlotte said, and for a moment they all just looked at each other, their curiosity plain.

"But that's it," Alison said. "Oh, and I had him over for dinner last night. We had a great time. As far as bringing him around so you can meet him, that's not going to happen."

"Well, I guess we could just come over there," Suzanne said. "Hey, Jenny, what do you think Ryan will do when he hears about the hunky neighbor Alison's spending time with?"

She just stared at her aunt in horror. "Don't you dare tell my dad," she said.

Both Charlotte and her mom laughed, and Alison knew Suzanne was enjoying this way too much.

"Oh, don't worry, Alison," she said. "I'm just messing with you. But I think you should invite your mom and Charlotte and me over so we can meet him. If you do that, we might just not tell your dad about him for, say, another week?"

The way Suzanne said it, she realized her family weren't about to let her have any time alone with Bennett like a normal family would.

"That's just cruel, Suzanne," she said. "It's not even serious. You're going to scare him away."

Suzanne just slid her gaze over to Jenny and then Charlotte before shaking her head. "I don't think so. The guy I saw didn't seem like the type who scared off easily."

Alison pulled in a breath, considering. She looked down at Cameron before passing him to Suzanne and glancing over at Charlotte. "If you want me to pick up Eva, I can," she started. "But hear me out. Bennett is someone I just met, so, if you don't mind, I'd rather not have the entire O'Connell family showing up and getting in his business."

Jenny nodded and rested both her hands on the island, leaning down. "You're right, Alison. No need to scare him away. But the thing is, once Ryan hears about him, you know he's going to show up…"

"And then Marcus will run a background check on him," Charlotte cut in.

"And Harold will likely talk to anyone who knows him," Suzanne said.

"So don't you think it's better if we meet him instead?" Jenny finished.

Alison realized she couldn't say no. "Fine, but you're cornering me. It will be a short meeting. Come over for tea and say hi when he has a day off, after I see him again. You're not allowed to embarrass me or say anything that will make it awkward, because I just met him. I like him, and I want a chance to get to know him."

She took in her mom and aunts. Even Cameron was looking at her now, happy and smiling.

"Great, can't wait to meet him!" Suzanne said.

But Alison realized this was just the beginning. Once Bennett had met her mom and aunts, the next set of O'Connells would be knocking on the door.

Eight

It was dark by the time Alison made it home. After Suzanne dropped her off, she made her way across the courtyard, looking up to the third floor, seeing her light on, and breathing a sigh of relief. It was something she didn't want to tell anyone about, and she wondered why she'd always been so scared of the dark.

She started up the concrete stairs, gripping her keys in her pocket, feeling the winter cold. She had spent family night at Marcus and Charlotte's, and the entire family, as always, had been there—minus Marcus and Harold, who seemed to have their hands full with a day of assaults. Thankfully, Charlotte, her mom, and Suzanne had said nothing about Bennett to her dad. At least she was grateful for that.

She stopped at her door, glancing over to Bennett's and hearing the quiet, wondering whether he was home or at work. A med student with crazy hours… She took a step and then another, then fisted her hand and knocked, the entire time telling herself this wasn't okay. She listened and didn't hear anything for a moment, and she felt like an idiot as she stepped away—but then she heard a clatter and footsteps before the door pulled open, and there he was in sweats and a T-shirt, appearing as if he'd just woken up.

"I'm so sorry. Did I wake you?" she said. "I was just getting home and saw your door…" She sounded so much like an idiot.

"Hey, Alison," he said. "No—yeah, sorry. Just crashed early…" There was a faint light on inside, and she couldn't really see much before he stepped out and pulled the door closed behind him. "Sorry, my place is a mess. Like, really. You don't even want a peek in there, because then you'd be horrified and would start giving me really odd looks. Messy guy? No, thanks." There was that sense of humor that had her lips pulling into a smile that wouldn't leave any time he was around.

Why was it that even when she was intruding on him, he made it sound like no big deal?

"So what's up?" he asked.

She noted he was barefoot and shivering, and she suddenly felt so awkward for him. "I was just getting home from my uncle's house. All the family was there for dinner and stuff. Just wanted to say hi. Boy, hearing me say it now and seeing that I woke you up, I feel like shit. Maybe, if we're both off tomorrow, you want to share dinner or a bite of something? That is, considering I'm not sure I even have a job anymore."

He crossed his arms, taking her in. "Did something happen? Did that shithead boss of yours fire you?" He was moving his feet side to side on the cold cement, not exactly comfortable. She expected him to say bye and go back inside his place, but he didn't.

"No, nothing like that. He was actually attacked, found in the cold food storage. Apparently, someone hit him, dragged him behind some boxes to hide him, and left him there, unconscious. He was hurt pretty bad, and the restaurant was closed today while they investigate. Haven't heard when it will reopen or how my boss is doing. Just one of those days, you know," she said. "I should let you get back inside. I didn't mean to drag you out in the freezing cold."

He gestured behind him. "Hey, why don't I just throw on a sweatshirt and pull on my shoes, and I'll come over and we can talk in your neat and tidy place?"

She couldn't help laughing. There it was, that interest and ease. She took in his tall, lanky build. What was it about him that seemed so perfect?

"Yeah, sure," she said. "I'll leave the door open."

He strode back into his place and closed the door quickly again before she could see in, and she started to hers, pulling her keys out. She shoved them in the lock. Was it odd that he didn't want her to see his place? She got the mess thing to a point, but this was ridiculous. She opened her door just as her cell phone rang, and she pulled it out, seeing her dad's caller ID. For a moment, she wondered who had sold her out, her mom or Suzanne.

"You know, I just got home," she said. "I saw you less than twenty minutes ago…"

"Hey, kiddo," Ryan said. "I just wanted to give you a heads-up. Apparently, your boss is awake at the hospital. Marcus was just there, talking with him and his wife. Chad says he doesn't know what happened. He was in the cooler late after closing last night, and he says someone must have hit him from behind, but he doesn't remember any of it. He's got quite a head injury, and he's confused. That was all Marcus said. The doctors had to do some emergency surgery for swelling or something. They're surprised he woke up at all, but he's in and out. They're saying it's a miracle, considering how hard he was hit and how long he was out.

"Hunter's there too after being run down. Apparently, he has a fractured arm and leg, cracked ribs, and a concussion. And, Alison, you should know I just heard the fire department were called out to Amanda's place. Remember her from school? There was a gas leak or something. Marcus hasn't been home yet. He called me because this is one too many in a suspicious string of assaults. He has no leads yet, no idea whether it's random or someone is messing with people. I would feel better if you came home, at least for tonight. I can swing over and pick you up."

Alison heard a tap on her open door behind her, and Bennett stepped inside in a navy sweatshirt, his feet shoved in sneakers. He closed the door but hesitated a second, seeing that she was on the phone. She just waved for him to come in.

"You know what, Dad?" she said. "I'm fine. Don't worry. I actually have a friend who's just come over. If it would make you feel better, I'll call you in the morning."

Would her dad let it go? Maybe he'd insist on coming over. She hoped not.

"First thing in the morning, you call or I'll be there, knocking on your door," Ryan said.

As she hung up, she couldn't help thinking about the difference between him and Wren. No wonder her mom had never been so happy.

"Everything okay?" Bennett said.

Alison rested her phone on the side table and took in her warm apartment, shrugging out of her coat. She pulled open the front closet and reached for a hanger. "Yeah, that was just my over-worrying father calling to give me a heads-up on my boss. It seems weird stuff is happening today, and he wanted me to move home for the night so he could stop worrying."

She wasn't sure what to make of Bennett's expression. She hung her coat in the closet and pulled the door closed, then strode into her kitchen. "Do you want something to drink?" she asked as she pulled open her fridge, not sure what was left, considering they'd polished off the last of the orange soda the night before. "Let's see… I have apple juice and—oh, a full carton of milk. Or there's water."

She took in his amusement as he shook his head and said, "You know, water works for me. And not everyone has a parent who calls to check in and care. That's nice."

She reached for two glasses in her cupboard and then turned to Bennett, not sure what to make of his remark. "I know. It's just so new still, my dad…" She gestured vaguely.

He nodded. Of course, he remembered. She wondered if it was having just woken up that made him seem like a different person, more pensive tonight. She filled the glasses and then walked over to the sofa, where he took a seat and lounged in the corner, sprawling out as if making himself at home. As he reached for the glass, he didn't pull his gaze from her. His eyes were blue mixed with hazel, which added to his hotness and branded him as so damn unique.

"Sit, Alison, and tell me about this dramatic turn of events today," he said. "So your boss is out, and your father is worrying, yet you still have that gorgeous smile. Seems as if everything isn't all that bad."

The way he said it, she had to fight the urge to go and look in the mirror to see what he found appealing about her smile. That was something no one had ever said to her.

"You know, you have a way of saying all the right

things," Alison said. "Even though this could've been a truly crappy day, you make a girl feel appreciated."

He appeared amused and laughed softly under his breath, but he said nothing.

"So my boss, in the hospital…apparently, he woke up briefly," she said. "He talked to my uncle Marcus, who is the sheriff, and—"

"Your uncle is the sheriff?" Bennett was now sitting up, and he put his glass on the old nicked sofa table, a hand-me-down from Suzanne.

"Yeah. Didn't I tell you that?" she said.

He was shaking his head, maybe a little unsettled. "No, you left out that little detail. Wow, that must be handy. So you said your boss woke up. Does he know who did it?" He stared at his water, then lifted the glass and took a swallow.

"No," she said. "That was why my dad called. He said that he doesn't remember much. He was hit pretty hard, a head injury bad enough they had to do surgery. They didn't expect him to wake up, but he did for a bit. He couldn't offer much, though, so they have no idea who did it or what happened. Then there's this guy I went to high school with, Hunter. Apparently, someone tried to run him down today. He's hurt pretty bad, in the hospital…"

"And did he see who did it?" Bennett cut in before she could go on, dragging his gaze to her, his forearms resting on his knees as he leaned forward. What was it about the way he was looking over to her? There was curiosity, an edge—something. He took another drink.

"No, my dad heard that he didn't see who it was. Just weird, is all. But what prompted his call was someone else from my old school, Amanda. Along with Hunter and a few others, she tried to pin something on me once. My dad said there was, like, a gas leak or something at her house today. I have no love lost for any of them, but hearing about Hunter and Amanda, I have to tell you…that was the first time I felt there was such a thing as karma. I had to tell myself it wasn't okay to feel that sense of satisfaction, but I wanted to thank the person who did what they did. Then I felt bad for thinking that way. What kind of weirdo gets off on that kind of vengeful thinking?"

She couldn't believe she'd said that.

He looked straight ahead, and the edges of his lips pulled up in a smile before he dragged his gaze over to her. "You're not a weirdo, Alison. It's called being human. Everyone thinks that way when someone screws them around, and having those thoughts is okay until you act on them. You didn't do it, obviously."

The way he said that had her remembering her uncle's worry, his reprimand to watch her mouth because of the trouble she could land them in.

"Ah, no, I didn't," she said. She was gripping her own water glass, wondering what he was thinking.

He stood, and after downing his glass, he rested it on the sofa table and groaned. "Then don't worry about any of it. None of this is your responsibility, but it sounds to me like just maybe, someone's looking out for you. I'm going to take that as my cue and turn in. I've got an early shift. Lock the door up behind me, and remember, I'm just next door. The walls are thin. Just give a knock on your bedroom wall, which is right next to mine, and I'll come running. I'm a light sleeper."

He walked to the door and pulled it open, but he gestured to the deadbolt and chain. "You know, this is pretty flimsy. You want to pick up a new deadbolt at the hardware store? I can change it out for you like I did mine. The only problem with a rental is that you have no idea how many keys are out there for your place," he said. Then he stepped out.

She pushed the door closed behind him and locked it, slipping the chain on. She stared at the lock, feeling suddenly nervous, because she'd never once considered someone else having a key to her place other than the manager. She paused at the realization that Bennett now knew the layout of her apartment. And that comment he'd made about someone doing her a favor?

"Right, that was weird," she said.

There was something about Bennett that she couldn't put her finger on—but then, if he liked her, he couldn't be entirely normal.

CHAPTER
Nine

Alison's cell phone was ringing as she blinked in the morning light. She sat straight up, pulled from a dream and a deep sleep, and tossed back the quilt to stumble from bed and hurry out to the living room in her nightshirt.

She'd left her cell phone plugged in and charging on the kitchen table, and she landed on it, seeing her dad's name on the screen.

"What time is it?" she snapped, though she saw the clock on the stove read 7:36 a.m. She felt the morning chill and pulled a hand over her face.

"Late," Ryan said quite sharply. "Remember when I said to call me in the morning?"

She could hear the edge in his tone, and she thought she heard her mom say something in the background as she walked over to the thermostat and turned it up. She shivered. "It's the crack of dawn, Dad, seriously. I was still asleep. I would've called you when I woke up."

She took in the door to her apartment and the chair she'd propped under the door handle before bed because of what Bennett had said about the number of keys that could be floating around out there. There was something about the light of day now; she was glad no one was there to see the chair and her paranoia.

"Well, now you're awake," Ryan said. "I just wanted to give you a heads-up about Amanda and the gas leak last night. Marcus stopped in a minute ago, and it seems it wasn't accidental. He didn't elaborate but said there were signs of foul play again. I don't know all the specifics, but hearing my brother and seeing his face, I can tell he's not taking this lightly. I know you said you're fine, but I'm not liking what I'm hearing. These aren't random strangers, Alison, so I'm about to get in my truck and come over there. I'm not kidding when I say I would feel more comfortable with you back here, even just for a few nights until Marcus and Harold have a handle on this and figure out who has an axe to grind. Marcus has never seen so many incidents in the span of a couple of days like this— and remember, kiddo, we've been in the spotlight way too much lately for my liking."

Alison walked across the pale carpet, back to her bedroom, and flicked on the beside lamp before reaching into her closet for her fluffy blue and white flowered robe. She pulled the phone away and put it on speaker before tossing it on her bed, then shrugged on her housecoat. She wished for a few more hours of sleep, but the cold was bringing her fast awake.

"Dad, I'm fine here, and I wouldn't be more comfortable at your place. There's a lock on my door, you know. Why are you worrying about me when it has nothing to do with me? Chad, Amanda, and Hunter are not me. You should be worrying about them, wondering what they did and who else they screwed around."

She knew she lacked any empathy in her tone as she

pulled open her drawer and reached for her socks, the thick, warm, fluffy ones. She pulled them on and picked the phone back up. "You're starting to sound a little paranoid, Dad. Are you suggesting it's the same person going after all three? I mean, logically, and I can't believe I'm saying this, but I'm sure Hunter and Amanda have a lot of other enemies after what they were part of. Every one of that crowd has an axe to grind with each other. And Chad isn't exactly boss of the year. So someone went after him? It's not me they're coming after, and I'm sorry they were hurt, of course, but at the same time, I'm not totally broken up about it."

There was silence for a moment. Why couldn't she feel any empathy for them?

"I seriously hope you don't go repeating that to anyone," Ryan said, "because it makes you sound guilty."

She let the phone slip away from her mouth as she stared at her open bedroom door. The blinds were tightly closed over the window behind her bed. She knew she really needed to stop spouting off about this, but with the odd way those three had been targeted, even she had to admit it seemed like someone was setting the record straight.

"Got it, Dad," she said. "I won't say anything else about it—but again, logically, don't panic. It just seems as if karma is at play here."

"Ha-ha, very funny," he said. "It's not like you to be logical about anything or talk about karma, but good for you. Regardless, when my brother calls and tells me to bring you home because he has an odd feeling he can't explain, I'm listening. I have that feeling now too, and I don't believe this is random, not by a long shot. It's too coincidental, and I'm going to quote Marcus on this, because he's right: There really is no such thing as a coincidence. So until we know what's going on and who's behind this, your mother and I would feel better with you here."

The way her dad said it had her taking in her place, feeling the freedom she didn't want taken away. She sighed heavily. From her nightstand drawer, the piece of light blue cloth she used to clean her cell phone screen caught her eye, and she pulled it open to find her red journal, a bookmark sticking out of it. She didn't know why, but it seemed out of place. She stared at it and then up, taking in her dresser and jewelry box and two snow globes, a Christmas village and Tinkerbell, as well as the dorky piggy bank she'd had since she was just a kid, which was filled with coins. It was something Wren had started, and she'd never parted with it. She ran her hand over the dresser, not sure what she was looking for.

"Come on, kiddo," Ryan said. "I'm pretty sure the restaurant is still closed today, so come and hang out with your mom and Charlotte. Help with the campaign. Then I can head out on the trail today without worrying that something could happen to you."

She pulled out her journal, looking at the bedside table, wondering what looked off. Had someone been in her room? She shut her eyes as soon as the paranoid thought entered her head. It was just her dad getting to her, and Bennett the night before, too.

"Dad, all this talk and worry from you and Uncle Marcus is only going to freak everyone out, including me, so stop it, already," she snapped, lifting her hand as if he could see it. "I'm fine. I'll text Nan about the restaurant and find out what's going on, see if she has any idea what's what, but I'm perfectly fine here in the meantime. What do you think is going to happen to me, anyway?"

In the silence that followed, she found herself gripping her book against her chest, trying to shake off that building anxiety in her stomach. She sat back on the bed and opened the book to the marked tab, seeing the list of names she'd written. She just stared without a clue what to say. Then she hissed, feeling the alarm jolt right through her. Her heartbeat kicked up, and she could feel the dampness along her back.

"Alison, what is it?"

Evidently, her dad had heard her.

She stared at the names, then back to the drawer, before shutting her eyes, feeling that wave of something that could see her getting in trouble for something she didn't do. "Nothing," she said. "It's nothing, just…the way you're going on is messing with my head, Dad. Stop putting all you and Marcus's paranoid crap on me. But I'll come and help today with the campaign, and I'll think about staying over."

Her dad sighed, and she didn't know why.

She stared again at the names of everyone she was furious with and thought of why she'd written them down. This was where she wrote her thoughts, her feelings. She understood well why she'd done it, but anyone else who saw this very private book would've been looking at her as a suspect. She stood up again, having to move because there was no way she was going back to sleep now. She held the book against her and reached for her phone on the bed.

"You sure you don't want me to swing by now?" Ryan said. "I can stop on my way in to work."

Her heart was thudding as she stepped out of the bedroom, seeing the locked front door with the chair still there under the knob. She found herself shaking her head, because who would understand why she'd made a list of everyone she hated? No one.

"Nope, I'm good, Dad," she finally said, wanting to get

off the phone, wanting to figure out what to do, needing to settle her nerves.

"Fine," he said. "I'll have your mom swing by and pick you up later."

Then her dad said goodbye and hung up, and Alison took in her living room, her neat kitchen. She settled her phone on the counter, realizing her hand was shaking.

She walked back into her room. The drawer beside her bed was now wide open, and she pulled the book she was still gripping away from her and opened it again to the list of names. Chad, Hunter, Amanda... Then there was Belinda, and she looked at the name that had been crossed out and circled in red: Cassie.

She ripped out the page and then took in her room again as she tried to figure out whether someone had been in there. The bookmark had been sticking out of the book at an angle, she thought, and the cloth had been caught in the closed drawer even though she didn't remember using it.

Everything in her place was neat and tidy and organized, but as she took in the open drawer, she realized she couldn't remember clearly how she'd left it. Either way, she couldn't shake the feeling, as she turned around, that someone was watching her.

Someone had been there, and someone knew something about her that she never would've shared with anyone.

CHAPTER
Ten

"You haven't said two words to me since I picked you up," Jenny said. "And I noticed you climbed in without an overnight bag. You know, when your dad called and said you weren't taking it seriously, I wanted to drive over and pack a bag for you. I understand this independence thing, wanting a place of your own, but as your mother, I'm worried. Marcus came knocking this morning after working really, really late and told us what's been going on. Even though it doesn't have anything to do with you, I can't shake this feeling that something bad is coming our way, considering our family seems to attract bad things over and over. Marcus never worries about little things, so if he says he's concerned and to pull you close, that's exactly what we're going to do."

Jenny gripped the steering wheel of the Jeep, and Alison thought back to how she had paced and circled her apartment, standing before her bedside table at least a dozen times, knowing the red book was still there, the page she'd ripped out tucked back inside it.

"Mom, I kind of have a lot on my mind. I was really

put out that Dad had to show up and co-sign on the apartment, vouching that I'll pay my rent and won't wreck the place, as if people think I'm completely irresponsible. Now some psycho is running around, taking out my boss, and there's Hunter and Amanda, too. When I texted Nan, she texted right back to say the restaurant is closed until further notice. I need money to pay my rent, so now I'm wondering if I need to start looking for another job. Am I even going to be paid for the hours I'm owed? So, yeah, I'm kind of pissed, Mom, because my peaceful, quiet world has been turned upside down. Just when I thought things were starting to look up…wham! Right up the back of the head. How is what happened to Chad, Hunter, and Amanda coming back on me? Like, what is this?"

The knot twisted in her stomach as she thought of everything that had been perfect yesterday and now suddenly wasn't. She hadn't done anything, but she couldn't shake the unreasonable feeling that she was responsible. She had to force herself to look out the window, feeling miserable.

As her mom pulled into their driveway, she spotted her dad's ranger's truck and another vehicle she didn't recognize.

"I didn't think Dad was home," she said. "Why isn't he working?" She knew she sounded accusing. She stepped out in her new skinny blue jeans and black V neck sweater under her winter coat, her makeup fresh, suddenly feeling as if she were twelve. It was a feeling she didn't much like.

"I don't know," her mom said as she stepped out and closed the door. Alison took in her puzzled expression before the door to the house opened—and there was her grandma, whom she hadn't seen in forever.

"Grandma! I didn't know you were coming back," she

said. She turned to her mom, who had an odd smile. "You knew, didn't you?"

Jenny just shrugged. "Yeah, but we didn't say anything because your dad said your grandma wanted to surprise you."

She strode up the steps, taking in her grandma's short dark hair, which was exactly the same. She was slim, wearing a cream sweater and blue jeans. When she held her arms out to Alison, she walked right into them, feeling the embrace, the love. She shut her eyes a second, feeling so grateful that she was here now.

Then her grandma pulled back and really looked at her, putting her hands on the sides of her face, holding her cheeks, and then brushing back her hair. "Oh, I missed you. I swear you get prettier every time I see you. And what's this I hear about you trying to grow up way too fast? Don't you know that I need you to stay young for me just a little longer, to need me and not grow up and live on your own?" Iris sighed and stepped back, and though Alison rolled her eyes, she felt the unconditional love that had always been there with her grandma. Iris slid an arm around her shoulder.

"Oh, Grandma, who says I don't still need you?" she said, then pulled in a breath as she saw her dad inside with Raymond, a.k.a. Jake, her grandfather, Brady's father. She wasn't sure how to feel about him. She knew her grandma was happy, but at whose expense? Hers.

She was pulled inside the house, hearing Marcus as well. He started talking with Raymond as Ryan began walking her way.

Something was wrong.

"Ryan, what's going on?" Jenny said.

Her dad stopped right in front of her, lifted her chin, and rested his hand on her head to rustle her hair a bit.

The knot in her stomach returned like a vice once again as he said, "Cassie's in the hospital."

Jenny gasped behind her, and Alison felt her grandma's arm around her, pulling her closer, holding her tight.

"She was coming down the stairs in her apartment," Ryan continued, "and someone was there, hiding, getting ready to hit her with a baseball bat. She saw it swing and managed to step away, but she turned and fell off the bottom step. It hit the wall behind her before she felt it come down on her. Apparently, whoever it was got a couple good licks in on her back and arm before running out. She had rolled and tried to get out from under it. Pretty sure if she hadn't moved so quick, she would've been hurt much worse—or killed. So, Alison, you can argue all you want, but until they find out who this is, you're moving back in here."

Alison stared at Raymond and Marcus, who both appeared grim. Her knees suddenly felt weak. "I need to sit down," she said, then pulled away from her grandma and sat down on the stairs, putting her head in her hands, just covering her face for a second.

Chad, Amanda, Hunter, and now Cassie. This didn't seem real. It was as if someone was reading her thoughts. Brady had to be beside himself. He was going to hate her.

"Alison, look," Marcus said. "I know you're worried, and you should be. We all need to step up things. No one is alone anymore. You move back in just until we can find out who this is, if it's personal or random. We don't know, but we'll find out…"

Raymond was watching her, and her grandma was leaning against the rail, so close to her, looking down, offering a lopsided smile that was kind of sad. She took them all in, wondering at what point she would finally drive them away. One by one, they would hate her. Her eyes burned as she looked up and over to her mom and dad, then back to her grandma. Then she shut them again, feeling sick. She could feel herself trembling.

"Hey, listen," Ryan said. "I know you're scared, but nothing is going to happen to you here."

She knew she needed to say something, but she couldn't get her tongue to move.

"So how is Cassie?" Raymond said, looking right at her. "How bad is she hurt?"

Did he have any idea what she'd done, what she was thinking, the things she'd written? She had to look away.

"She's banged up, and Brady is out of his mind with worry," Marcus said. "They're going to bunk in at Mom's. I spoke with Chad's wife this morning. Seems they were separating, so I'm looking at that. I've been trying to track down Belinda since last night to find out whether something went down between her and Chad the night before, but she's not answering. I've tried getting a hold of her parents, the Lees, but they're down in Florida right now. I know Harold is heading over to her house again. He's been trying to reach Mr. Lee to get permission to go in the house, but I've asked him to get a warrant in case we don't hear back. I'm already betting they'll say no to letting us just walk into their house and talk to their daughter. I have to say that because Belinda just started working for Chad, and now she's missing, she's looking good for this. She knew Hunter, who was just working at a car wash as part of his probation, and Amanda. But she doesn't even know Cassie… I mean, this is totally out of left field."

Alison just stared at her uncle, the sheriff, whose cell phone was now ringing. He turned away as he answered it. She remembered his face when he'd warned her to watch her smart mouth, and she felt the hole she was digging for herself by not saying anything. Her mom and dad were beside themselves with worry.

Her grandma reached out and touched the top of her head. She looked up to her, seeing how much she loved her. Would she feel the same way if she knew the thoughts she never should've written down? But her journal was private and personal… *What the fuck?*

"Hey, what's going on?" Raymond said.

She had to remind herself that Brady's father was her grandfather, too, and then she couldn't help wondering who he would love more. She lowered her gaze, working her fingers, twisting the ring on her middle finger with the flower, which she never took off.

"This may sound totally weird," she said. "It sounds completely nuts even to me…but I have this journal. I write all my personal thoughts in it." She could feel her throat wanting to close and her heartbeat kicking up. She had to force herself to look up, hoping Belinda was good for this. But she couldn't shake the creepiness she had felt that morning. "You're all going to hate me…" She pressed her hands to her face, not wanting to look up.

"Hey, no one is going to hate you," Ryan said. "Look at me. It doesn't matter what you do, Alison, not ever…" He was holding her mom's hand tightly, and everyone was looking down at her except Marcus, who was still on the phone in the kitchen. Good. She didn't want the sheriff hearing what she had to say.

"What does your journal have to do with what's happened?" Raymond finally asked.

She wondered now why she hadn't burned that page, why she had just shoved it back in the drawer. "Because I made a list of everyone I hated, of everyone who had hurt me. I write down my feelings in private…and I think someone read it."

Her dad made an odd face as if he didn't believe her. Her mom was staring at her with a look she hadn't seen in a long time, and her grandma… She didn't want to look up to and see the horror she knew would be there.

Raymond didn't pull that shrewd, hard gaze from her. Those O'Connell blues seemed filled with the kind of fire and warning she'd never wanted to be on the wrong side of. "And is Cassie on that list?" he asked.

She thought she heard her mom gasp. She forced back the lump in her very dry throat and nodded.

"And Chad, Hunter, Amanda…" Raymond said matter of factly.

She could only nod to each name. Her voice had failed her. She wondered when she was supposed to feel better for telling them what a fuckup she was.

"I see. Well, then, I guess we have a problem. Anyone else on the list?" Raymond sounded so calm, and he didn't look away. She wished he would.

"Belinda Lee," she said.

Just then, Marcus walked back into the room, and her stomach twisted tighter. She couldn't remember having seen her uncle look so grim. He pulled his hand over his face and made a sound of defeat. "That was Harold. I guess we can rule out Belinda having been behind this."

Her ears were ringing as she stared over to her uncle, who still didn't have a clue what she'd done.

"She was found dead in her bathtub," he said, then looked right at her. "Drowned."

She wanted to go home.

Everyone downstairs by the door had stared at her with that look she never wanted to see, the kind of horror she didn't think she'd ever get past. She needed a corner to hide away from everyone. Even though she was part of this family, she wished for anonymity instead of the judgement that would soon come down on her. She knew full well that everyone had to be thinking she'd finally gone too far.

Maybe that was why she'd slipped away upstairs into the bathroom and locked the door, climbing into the bathtub with her clothes on, feeling the cold porcelain against her and only hearing the distant murmur of voices.

She was pretty sure no one had noticed as she slipped away, or maybe they didn't really care. They were likely happy she was gone. She squeezed her sweater, which covered her heart, not sure she could remember ever having felt this horrible ache, even after Wren and everything that had happened—the lies, the secrets, when the man she'd believed to be her father had thrown the truth in her face in a drunken stupor. The memory came back to her so vividly, so painfully.

Then there was Ryan O'Connell. She'd always believed there would be a point where he and all the O'Connells would wash their hands of her, saying, "You're just too difficult," "We can't have you here," "You're not one of us."

This, she believed, was that moment. The final straw.

There was a knock at the old white door, and she just stared at it, sitting lower in the bathtub, saying nothing. Her heartbeat pounded long and loud, the thump now echoing in her ears. She couldn't remember a time that she hadn't been scared.

"Alison, I know you're in there. Come on, honey. Open up."

She shut her eyes, hearing Raymond's voice. Of course he'd be the one to come up, maybe to point out to her how badly she'd screwed up again, to tell her she had to go and how much he hated her for hurting his son.

Brady… It killed her now, thinking of the hate that would be in his eyes for her.

She said nothing, feeling abandoned. She didn't move and had no intention of answering, but she heard a click, and then the door opened. Her heart zigged and her stomach zagged as she bolted upright, staring at a man she didn't know how to feel about.

He took in the bathroom, with its single sink and oval mirror, white walls and green towels, and the bathtub she was sitting in. She pulled her knees up as he closed the door, his hand on the knob, likely considering where to start. Her eyes burned from the tears she'd cried, and she quickly pulled her fingers under them, swiping away the smudges of mascara. She knew her face was a mess.

She said nothing as she swallowed the thick lump,

knowing he was Brady's father and he was likely wondering how a freak like her could be in their family.

"I can see by your face that you're a little freaked and a lot upset over what happened," he said. "I can understand it."

He leaned back against the sink and crossed his arms over his dark green long-sleeved shirt. He was in blue jeans and had thick dark socks on his feet, and his dark hair was short and wavy, with flecks of white weaving their way through.

Still she said nothing. Her throat was dry, and she didn't think she had the energy for speaking. She leaned back against the bathtub, pulling her arms tighter around her, fisting the sleeves of her sweater. It was all she could do to hang on.

He pulled in a breath. "You know, Alison, no one blames you here."

"Of course they do. You do. You hate me. Everyone does," she snapped, hearing the bitchiness come through. That had always been her go-to every time she felt cornered.

"No, Alison. I'm upset, we all are, but I'm at a loss for what to say to you to make this situation not as horrible as it is. So you wrote some hateful words. Who doesn't? We all have someone we hate."

She just stared at him, wondering what was coming next. This had to be a trick. She was still waiting for him to point out to her what an awful human being she was. Then maybe she could go back to figuring out how to slip out of this house and get home to her place, where she could lock the door and keep everyone out.

Then there was Bennett. Would he feel the same way about her if he knew what she had done? She ached, thinking that even her traitorous thoughts were something anyone could take from her. Maybe that was why she couldn't shake this feeling of having been violated.

"No one hates you," Raymond said. "Everyone downstairs is only interested in making sure you're okay and that you stay okay—you and everyone else in this family."

She just stared at him, because nothing he said could make her believe him. He watched her and then looked away. She hoped he'd leave. How long would she have to sit here and hide until she found the courage to climb out of the bathtub and walk down the stairs and out the front door?

Would anyone stop her?

"I don't know what to say to you, Alison, to make this better for you. I can't even imagine the horror you must be feeling, violated, hurt, angry. There is no greater violation than someone reading your private journal, your very private thoughts, which you have a right to."

She had to look away and pressed her lips together, staring at the faucet of the bathtub, because she didn't want to hear this from him. He sat down on the closed toilet, closer to her, and pressed his hand to her head.

A tear slipped out, but she slapped her face, pulling roughly, quickly, so he wouldn't see it.

"Do not under any circumstances be angry with yourself here," Raymond said. "At the same time, I need to ask you something."

There it was. She knew something would be coming, and she'd have to explain why she did what she'd done, though she had no intention of ever explaining it to anyone.

"What?" she cried. "You mean why I wanted to hurt Cassie and everyone, why I'm responsible for killing someone?"

She hated Belinda, but she hated herself more for

feeling the way she did right now. Everyone would know how guilty she was—and she couldn't shake the imagined image of Belinda dead in a bathtub.

"You didn't do anything wrong, and you certainly didn't kill anyone," Raymond said. "All you did was write things down, names. You wrote what bothered you instead of keeping it bottled up." He gestured to her, and she stared at him suspiciously. "That is what you did, right?"

She hesitated only a second, then nodded.

"Well, okay then. You need to let yourself off the hook, Alison. This isn't on you, and no one is blaming you for this...but I need to see it. I'm asking you so we can figure out who did this. I don't understand why, but I stopped trying to figure out why people do the things they do a long time ago. Did someone break in? Have you shown anyone your journal or talked about it, or maybe you've shown someone the list of people you have issues with?"

She pulled in another breath, feeling the catch in her chest, feeling sick. There was no way she was letting anyone invade her personal thoughts again or read that book, see that list. Private and personal meant just that.

How well did anyone really know someone? Someone had read her very personal thoughts. When? Where? How? It felt completely unreal. She didn't think she'd ever get past this.

"I can see you're having trouble here, but you have to know, Alison, that as angry as you are at yourself, I'm more angry at myself," Raymond said. "I'm responsible in some ways. I'm so sorry for what I did to you and Brady. Seeing how hurt you were, I knew I was playing with fire. The problem with secrets is they blow up in your face. Cassie, though, is a nice girl..."

"I know she is!" Alison said. "What do you want me to say—that I shouldn't have thought it? I was angry. I'm sorry, but I can't help how I feel. No one is supposed to be reading my journal."

Raymond was shaking his head. "You think I don't know that? Everyone you wrote down is someone who hurt you in some way, am I right?" He linked his hands together. For a moment, it seemed as if this was a trick.

"I'm not showing you my journal. It's private." She knew she was being stubborn, but she wasn't letting anyone into her thoughts, sharing the kinds of things she put to paper just so she wouldn't bottle them up. She'd always done it so she wouldn't go crazy with the things in her head that had her hating everything about her life.

He only nodded and looked away, and she wondered what was coming next, because she didn't think this was the end of it.

"Brady is going to hate me," she said. He was the one person it killed her to think would never forgive her.

"Brady won't hate you," Raymond said. "No one is going to say anything, Alison. He won't know."

She made a rude noise. "Hey, you said it about secrets. They find a way out. You think I haven't been down this road before? Too many fucking times everyone has seemed to think they can talk about me, lie about me, make up stories about me, keep secrets about me, then throw them in my face when it can hurt me the most, and I'm supposed to just take it." She knew she was yelling, and she pulled in a breath, fisting her hands, taking in the shock or something in his expression.

"Why do I think we're not talking about your journal and what you wrote anymore?" Raymond finally said.

There was another knock at the door, and this time when it opened, there was Marcus in his sheriff's jacket. He looked at Raymond and then dragged his gaze over to her. His expression, the way he winced, made her shut her eyes and look away, across the old and dated tile.

"You ask her yet? Time is up," Marcus said.

She didn't know what passed between them. No one said anything, and she listened to the creak as Raymond stood up and moved away. Marcus squatted down and leaned on the bathtub right beside her, but she didn't want to look over.

"Alison, look at me," he said. Marcus could be so direct at times.

She sniffed loudly as she turned her head, pushing her heels on the bottom of the tub so she could sit up, leaning as far back in the corner as she could.

He was shaking his head, and she realized Raymond was still there, leaning against the sink, suddenly crowding her. This bathroom wasn't made for entertaining, but here they were. "All I can say is that one day, many years from now, you may look back on this moment and not want to crawl into a hole or pull the covers over your head. But that's not right now. I get it." He shook his head, his expression pensive. "I need to see the journal, the list of names."

She was already shaking her head and went to look away when he settled his hand on her shoulder.

"You think we don't all know the heavy dark cloud you carry? You've had the shit kicked out of you. We get it, and there isn't one of us in the family who hasn't wanted to go and exact justice for you, to protect you from everything else. But we can't. Right now, the only way I can stop this and figure it out is to see everything. You seem to think someone read your journal… Alison, this list of names changes nothing between us. You're family. You're stuck with us, and if you think running and hiding is the answer, I think you know by now that we're just going to run after you and look for you. If you don't already know that, then I'm really angry. There's nothing you could think or do that would make us love you any less. Come on. I need you to pull on those big-girl pants so we can figure out who's doing this. Your mom and dad and grandma are waiting for you to come downstairs. The only reason they're not up here right now is because we asked them to let us talk to you. You've got to forgive us, Alison."

She wondered whether her surprise showed in her face. "What does this have to do with you?" she said. "You didn't do anything. This was all me."

Raymond was shaking his head, and as Marcus stood up, she could see the lines around his eyes, see how tired he was. He held his hand out to her. "No, Alison, it's not on you. Come on, get up." He just stood there, unmoving, and didn't pull back. "I can wait you out, you know, but do you really think we have that kind of time?"

She let him take her hand and pull her up, and she wasn't sure what to make of his expression.

"Just one question before we go," Marcus said. "Can you think of anyone who would've had access to your place, to your journal? Is there anyone who could've been in your apartment? I already asked your mom and dad about the house here, but they swear no one would've been in your room, so it has to have happened at your apartment."

For just a moment, she thought of Bennett telling her to change the locks. His comment about her bedroom being next to his still bothered her. Everything about him seemed almost too perfect.

"Alison, what is it?" Marcus said.

She had to force herself to look up when there was no way she wanted to believe it. "Just Bennett," she said, then shrugged.

Marcus and Raymond exchanged the kind of odd look that had her stomach pitching again, that sick feeling that this was heading in a bad direction. She had met a good guy and thought her luck was finally turning, but now she would be Alison, the misfit who'd been screwed over, again.

"Who is Bennett?" Raymond asked.

She shrugged again and pulled her hand from Marcus's. "A guy I met at the restaurant. He lives next door to me."

"Let me guess. He's been in your apartment," Marcus said, and all she could do was nod.

Why did it seem that as soon as one good thing happened, something bad followed?

"But he wouldn't do this," she said.

The way Marcus, her uncle, suddenly became the sheriff looking down on her, she knew he didn't believe her.

Twelve

What was supposed to have been just Marcus and her going back to her apartment had suddenly turned into a three-ring circus. Her mom and dad had refused to let her walk out of the house without them, and now her grandmother was parked in the back seat of the Jeep beside her, with her mom driving and her dad in the passenger seat, giving directions as if she'd never been to the Carlyle before. To make it worse, he was still in his ranger's uniform, packing his gun. Marcus was following behind in the sheriff's vehicle, too, with Raymond.

Would she ever get her head around the fact that the man was her grandfather?

She'd glimpsed her face in the bathroom mirror for only a second, but she knew it was streaked with red blotches from dried tears and black smudges from her mascara. She'd have given anything for a minute just to clean up, but no one seemed inclined to let her amid the gravity of the situation.

She refused to look anyone in the eye, but she felt her

grandma reach over and grip her hand as they pulled up in front of her apartment. To her horror, there was a second cop car, occupied by Harold and Suzanne, Owen, and Tessa. She bolted forward, gripping the seat back in front of her, and she thought she hissed.

"Why is everyone here?" she snapped, staring out the front windshield.

At that exact moment, it seemed everyone saw her. She'd pulled her hand free from her grandma, who now ran it over her shoulder instead, and her dad looked back to her. Her mom was looking at her in the rear-view mirror, and she felt as though she were under a microscope.

"Everyone's worried about you, is all, nothing more," Jenny said.

"It's just family, Alison," her dad started in. "This is what we do…"

"But this is private and personal," Alison snapped. "What, did you tell everyone what I did? Oh, man, I'm such a fool. You're probably all waiting to tell me how I screwed up. Fine, I get it. Do you want me to say it? I suck. I'm an asshole. Is that what this is?"

She yanked on the door, but her grandma slapped her hand over her arm, holding her there. The strength in her grip was amazing. She gestured to the front. "Jenny, Ryan, give us a minute," she said in a tone Alison hadn't heard before.

She couldn't believe her mom and dad slipped out of the vehicle and closed the doors just like that. She stared at Marcus and Harold and her dad, mom, Suzanne, Tessa, and Owen, all gathering close. She didn't see Raymond and wasn't sure where he was.

"Alison, seriously, no one here is thinking any less of you," Iris said. "Your grandfather already told me that you think you're somehow responsible for this. You're not. This isn't your mess. Look at who's out there. That's your family, our family, and they're here for you. We're all sick with worry because none of us knows what to say to make this better. This kind of sick violation… I don't know if I would handle this any better than you, honestly. Do you remember when I was arrested? Do you remember that day?"

Her grandma was still holding her arm, and she slid her gaze over to her, seeing the kindness in her eyes. Iris was her go-to when everything crashed and burned, and that day had been one of the worst.

"Of course I do," she said. "How could I forget? That was an awful day, Grandma."

"And did you ever wonder what a horrible person I was, say you'd never speak to me again, or think less of me?"

She knew she made a face. "Now you're being ridiculous, Grandma. You didn't do anything wrong. You were railroaded, and…"

Her grandma angled her head and looked at her deeply. "I did kill a man, you know. But I did it to protect my family. You haven't answered me, though. I really feared that you and Eva would never see me the same way again… as a hero."

She had to pull in a breath, and she shrugged. "I could never think less of you, Grandma. You're my rock."

Her grandma, who'd been a part of her life for only a short time, made a face as if making a point. "Then why, dear girl, would you ever think for one moment that I could think less of you, especially where you are the victim here? I can't imagine how you must feel, thinking someone invaded your privacy and read your personal thoughts, which are yours alone." She gestured out the front windshield. "You see them, your family? They're right there, ready to support you no matter what, so don't start thinking the worst of them or yourself. They'd never think less of you. My kids, let me tell you, they tested me and did things they believe I still don't know about. But it doesn't change anything. We love each other, and that's that, so let yourself off the hook."

Then her door opened, and there was Marcus, his gun and badge visible, his gaze unwavering.

"Come on, Alison," he said. "Let's go, unless you want to hand me the keys and tell me where this book is, and I'll go and look."

She slipped out of the vehicle, pulling at her coat. "No, this is my place and my book. I seriously feel as if I'm naked here, so if you don't mind…"

Her uncle closed the door behind her with a shove as she strode onto the sidewalk, past her family. She felt her dad's hand on her shoulder, and then her mom slipped her arm around her and fell in beside her. Suzanne took up the other side. She hadn't expected this. Everyone else was climbing the stairs behind them all the way up.

As she pulled the keys from her pocket and slid them in the lock, she turned to glance at Bennett's door. Her dad touched her hand, took the key, and unlocked the door.

He stepped inside with Marcus and Harold, and she glanced back, seeing her grandma and Raymond bringing up the rear, looking around. Owen and Tessa were hand in hand, surveying the other apartment doors as well.

"Come on, Alison," Suzanne said, pressing a hand to her back and prodding her forward.

She stepped inside her apartment, taking a breath. She didn't know why, but she was slapped again with that paranoid feeling that had her rolling her shoulders. Her space had been invaded. This place, this apartment, which had been her sanctuary, now felt like anything but.

Everyone else followed her in, and the cool air drifted in through the open door. She kept walking, seeing her dad and uncle in her bedroom. The light was on there, and the bathroom one too. Harold looked at her, and she wanted to shrink back from his expression, but he reached out and rested his hand on the back of her neck and head, a supportive gesture, though he said nothing.

She strode past her dad and around her bed, which she'd made, to pull open the bedside drawer.

Marcus touched her hand to stop her. "What makes you think someone was in here?" he said.

She had to look at him, wondering if he thought she was crazy. "Just a feeling. I don't know. There was just something about the way I had left everything. I noticed a cloth sticking out of my drawer, the one I clean my cell phone screen with, but the thing is that I didn't leave it that way."

Her uncle was listening to her, standing tall, his hands on his duty belt. He gestured to the drawer.

"Are you going to say I'm crazy now?" she said.

"I'd never say you're crazy. If you have a feeling someone was in here, then someone was. End of story. When you notice something not looking right or have a feeling something is off, you should pay attention to it, because when you get that feeling, you're likely right. All I want to do is walk you through what you saw so I hear every little detail that could help me figure this out."

She nodded, then pulled the drawer open and reached inside for her red journal, which was lying sideways. She held it out to him, recalling every personal, private, inse-cure rambling thought she'd jotted down, and she cringed in horror that anyone would read that. Maybe he understood her worry, as he didn't pull his gaze as he touched her shoulder and held the book.

"Show me the page," he said, handing it back to her.

Her heart was pounding as she took in the book and flipped it open. She went through the pages, seeing the torn paper, but she couldn't find the page she'd stuck back in.

"It has to be here somewhere," she said. "I swear I ripped it out and shoved it right back in my journal."

She dropped the journal on the bed and rummaged in the drawer next, pulling out everything—extra cords for her phone, her kindle, her iPad, blank notebooks and pens. Then she stepped back, her hands up, her heard pounding. Her dad was watching her, her uncle, and she could see Raymond and Harold in the doorway.

She just shook her head. "I swear it was there, right there." She picked up the book and opened it up to the page that was missing.

"I believe you, Alison," Marcus said. He took the open book from her and glanced at it, then tilted it upside down, fanning the pages so anything loose would fall out.

"Dad, I put it back in there! I don't understand. Who would take it? It was here this morning before I left… How many hours ago? I'm not crazy." She could hear the pitch of her voice.

Her dad was right there, his hand on her shoulder. "No one is saying you are. I'm not liking this. Someone was in here again. Are they watching this place? Someone took the page. We're going to figure it out."

Marcus was still holding her journal, and he gestured to Harold. "What about this Bennett next door? I think maybe it's time we had a word with him. I want you to look around and see if anything else is missing."

She sat on her bed, feeling her knees weaken, and rested her face in her hands.

"Alison, I don't want you to worry," Ryan said. "We'll figure it out, but in the meantime, I also want you to pack a bag."

She looked over to Raymond and Harold, who gestured to Marcus and said, "And the front door? It doesn't look like anyone forced their way in, so whoever it was must have a key."

Raymond was looking right at her, and she remembered that feeling from the night before, the chair she'd slid under the knob.

"Yeah," she said. "Bennett said something about that last night to me. He asked me to pick up a new lock and said he'd change it. He mentioned something about the number of keys floating around and wondering who has them…"

Then Harold was gone, and Raymond with him. She heard her front door open and then heard the knock next door, and though she listened, expecting to hear something, she heard nothing.

"Okay, Alison," Marcus said. "I want you to tell me everything you know about this Bennett."

As she took in her uncle and her dad, all she could do was wonder why. Why did she continue to attract the worst of the worst people, places, and things?

Thirteen

Alison took in Karen's flowered dish set as she put away the plates that had dried in the rack, hearing Tessa and Owen from the sofa. Her mom was leaning on the counter not far from her, and she knew Suzanne had her hand in the bag of cookies she'd helped herself to from the cupboard.

"It may not even be him, you know," Jenny said.

Suzanne glanced toward her with an expression that was lacking the usual mischief. "If it is, I want first go at him," she said, then shoved another cookie in her mouth.

"You know," Owen called out from the couch, "it would've been nice if you'd told us about him. Marcus could have run a background check, and Ryan could have talked face to face with him, set some boundaries, and get a feel for him. Knowing he was in here, snooping around, Ryan is hanging by a thin thread, about ready to snap. Just thinking of what could've happened to you… He could have come in when you were sleeping."

Tessa jabbed Owen in the stomach with her elbow.

"Ow! What would you do that for?" he said.

Tessa shook her head and firmed her lips. "Because you don't go around saying things like that, Owen. It's not Alison's fault. None of this is."

"I put a chair under the door," Alison said.

Everyone was looking at her for a moment, and she wasn't sure they'd understood her, by the confusion that knit across Owen's face. He was the only male there right now, because her dad, Marcus, Harold, and her grandfather were outside…doing what, exactly? She wasn't sure.

She gestured to the door and then to a wooden dining chair. "I propped a chair under the doorknob before I went to bed last night because I was kind of freaked out after Bennett mentioned I should pick up a new deadbolt. He said he'd install it. He said in a place like this, keys tended to float around."

No one said anything. Great, another awkward moment. She felt her mom's hand on her arm.

"When your dad and Marcus come back up, we should go," Jenny said.

She dragged her gaze over to her mom but didn't say anything. Then she heard the front door open, and there were her dad and Marcus. Harold was outside with Raymond, she thought. Her grandma had just come out of the bathroom and flicked off the light, and she was looking over to Marcus and Ryan.

"So what's the verdict?" was all Iris said.

Ryan was shaking his head. He had gone down with Marcus to have a chat with Trish Huckman, the building manager. "Spoke with Trish about the locks. She said they don't change them when a tenant moves out. They get the keys back, and she says she's never had a problem. Of course, there are no security cameras anywhere, either. Marcus asked her how many keys there are and who has them, and she said

Alison has one and the owners have the other. She assured me there was no possible way others could be floating around, as tenants are specifically told not to copy them."

He walked over to the island, staring at her with a tired look in his eyes that she didn't want to dissect too closely. Everyone was watching them.

She heard her door again, and Harold strode in and said, "No one home next door. Knocked again and listened. Did you ask the landlady downstairs about getting us in?"

Marcus dragged his gaze from Harold over to her. "I asked Trish about Bennett. She said he hasn't lived there that long, is quiet, always pays his rent on time. She's had no issues with him. She didn't offer up much of anything else, and she said no to the key unless we have a warrant. Apparently, he drives a white Volvo, but I looked around the lot and didn't see it. You said he's a med student? So he's at the hospital."

Suzanne, standing right beside her, dug out another cookie from the bag and was about to take a bite when Raymond pushed open the door and poked his head in.

"I'm in next door," he called out.

She just stared. It took her brain a second to realize what her grandfather was talking about. He'd just broken into Bennett's apartment!

"I'm not sure how I feel about that," she said to Suzanne as Marcus and Ryan followed Harold out. She stopped listening to what they were saying. Her feelings for Bennett were taking a turn to something she was familiar with. "What reason would he even have to come into my place? This is ludicrous. You know what? All this is just making me paranoid."

What could she say? She couldn't wrap her head

around how it could possibly be Bennett. As she had time to think about it, it seemed impossible.

"Maybe," Suzanne said, "but from everything you said, Alison, even I agree it's starting to seem almost too good to be true."

"You mean because it's me, the fuckup, and how could anyone really, genuinely like me?"

"Alison, no one is saying that," Owen cut in, standing from the sofa beside Tessa. "Suzanne certainly isn't. Give yourself a break and try seeing yourself as we do. You said he's a med student. What else can you tell us about him? How many times have you had him in your apartment?"

She felt her mom slide her hand over her shoulder. "Owen, there's no way Alison could've had any idea he could be a problem," she said.

"Jenny," Ryan called out, pushing open the door again.

She realized her grandma was leaning there against the wall, so quiet, thinking. Her dad gestured, and her mom started walking. Something about his face had her chest squeezing, feeling that awful tightness again, which always came when something really bad was happening. She followed her mom, but Owen stepped over and put his arm out to stop her.

"Alison, stay here with Owen and Suzanne," Ryan said. "Mom and Tessa…"

She just shook her head, not pulling her gaze from her dad even though her mom had already stepped out of the apartment. "No, no more," she said. "This is about me. You're over in Bennett's place, calling for Mom, trying to keep something from me. I know when you're hiding something."

"Ryan, what is it?" Iris asked.

Ryan shook his head, and all she could see was worry

—and something else. "He's got pictures up on the wall, photographs of Alison, Jenny…"

She somehow pushed past Owen, and her dad grabbed her to stop her, holding her.

"I do not want you to see this!" he snapped.

"Dad, stop treating me as if I'll break. Please, I have to see…"

He let her go.

Harold was in the doorway, unsmiling, and she stepped past him into the apartment. Bennett had warned her it was a mess, but the carpet was clean. There was a small table, a few boxes, and photographs taped to the walls in the neat and tidy living room.

She took in Raymond, who was off to the side, and Marcus, but all she could see were images of her, some with her holding Eva's hand in the park, walking outside school, spanning a number of months. There were several of her mom and Wren. She took a step and then another, seeing the image of a man who'd terrorized her mother, who had loved her in a sick, twisted way.

She'd watched him bleed out on the floor after being shot. He was the man she'd believed was her father.

As she saw this here, now, a chill swept through her, numbing her. She felt a hand on her shoulder. It was Raymond, and he slid it around her and gestured to the wall.

"Who is that man in the photos?" he said.

She just stared at his image. "That's Wren Sweetgrass, my father," she said, then gave her head a shake as she looked over at Raymond. "The man I thought was my father, the man who raised me, that's him. Why? What is this?"

There were more photos of other people: Wren with another woman, dark skinned, beautiful, someone she'd never seen before. She took in the horror on her mom's face.

"Mom, who is that woman with Wren?" she asked, and she couldn't believe she sounded so calm.

Her dad came up behind her, rested his hands on her shoulders, and squeezed. Raymond stepped away, over to the photo of the other woman, whom she'd never seen before.

Her mom shrugged, alarm on her face, and she let out a sigh and turned as if at a loss. "I don't know," she said.

Just then, she heard a voice on the stairs outside—and she watched as Bennett strode in. The expression on his face was pure rage.

"What the hell are you doing in my apartment?" he snapped, his wool coat in his hand, gesturing at them. "Alison, what is this?" He sounded so accusing, and by the range of emotion on his face, she knew they were standing in the midst of a secret. She didn't have a clue who this guy was.

"I'd like to ask you the same thing," she said. "Why do you have pictures of me on your wall? My mom and my— and Wren, and the other woman in the photo with him?" She jabbed a finger to the wall, taking a step toward a man she had really liked and now was so angry at.

All he did was shake his head as he looked down at the floor. His expression wasn't that of a man who'd been caught. As she waited, he lifted his gaze and took in everyone in the room before letting it fall back on her, angling his head.

"Wren Sweetgrass was my father," he said, "and the woman in the photo with him is my mother. Now, what the hell are you all doing here?"

She couldn't pull her gaze from Bennett. "Did you plan

to meet me?" she said, taking another step toward him, but she felt her dad touch her arm.

She knew her family were trying to wrap their heads around this. He didn't answer, and he didn't pull that gaze from her. What was it about looking into those hazy blue eyes? She realized now what was familiar about them. They were Wren's.

He just shrugged, then looked over to Marcus. She knew he could see the sheriff's badge, and, of course, there was Harold by the door, too.

"I want you all to leave," he said. "You have a warrant to be in my place?"

There it was: the moment she knew this would all go sideways.

"The thing is, Bennett," Marcus said, "we're going to have to ask you to come down to the station. I have some questions about a list of names, a break-in at Alison's apartment, the assaults of Chad Hargrave, Cassie O'Con-nell, and Hunter Rowse, and the murder of Belinda Lee."

Then Marcus and Harold had Bennett pinned against the wall. He took a swing at Marcus, yelling, but they somehow cuffed him and pulled him out of the apartment, and all she could hear was him yelling, over and over, "I didn't do it!"

CHAPTER
Fourteen

She knew it was cold out, but she didn't care.

Alison sat on the front porch of her parents' house, hearing her family inside. Just as Marcus pulled up across the street, the front screen door opened, and she looked back to see her grandma stepping out in a white bomber jacket. She pulled the inside door closed behind her.

"Was wondering where you took off to," Iris said. Her smile had always made Alison feel better, until today.

She shrugged. "Just wanted to be alone and not have everyone looking at me, making me feel like shit, any more than I do right now. If I stay in there, I'm going to end up saying something to Brady and Cassie. She has no idea I'm responsible for her being nearly killed. Did you see the bruises on her, her face, the cast on her arm? How long does she have to wear that sling? She was having trouble even breathing... I can't look at her, so I figured I was better off out here, alone. She shouldn't be here. I know we're family, but she should've stayed in the hospital."

Iris pulled over the other metal deck chair and sat

beside her. She watched her uncle step out of his cruiser across the street. Tonight, everyone was here, and she knew it was because of her.

"I agree she should be, but they discharged her," Iris said. "This is where anyone in this family would be if we were hurt. Again, Alison, you're not responsible. Let it go. You had the shit kicked out of you again, but you don't have a corner on that. I swear, there was a time I didn't think I could take any more coming at me. But I got through it, and now I have the perfect family." She reached over and squeezed Alison's arm, her tone teasing.

She didn't know what to say at first. Her grandma, it seemed, was determined to sit vigil with her. "So what do you think happened with Bennett?" she finally said. "Did you see the pictures on the wall of his mother and Wren? So the entire time Wren was married to my mom, he had another kid… Was he playing house with her, too? Because I'm starting to think back and do the math on how much he wasn't there. Was he off with another woman? Mom said nothing, but I could see she was freaked out by it. Did she know about Bennett's mother? I mean, did Wren have a relationship with her? And Bennett…how did he know about me and my mom? Was he stalking me? The entire time, running into me over and over, was it all planned? Was he following me? The pictures were creepy—stalkerish creepy. I really liked him, you know. I was thinking my luck had finally turned and this good-looking guy was really into me. Do you have any idea how good I felt only to have the rug yanked out from under me again?" She let out a breath, feeling the ache and hearing her paranoia.

Her grandma seemed so pensive for a moment. "If there is one thing I know well, it's family secrets. There's nothing I can say to explain it, and we don't know the what, where, how, and why of it. Marcus and Harold will find out, though, and then we'll know. But your mom, no. She didn't know anything, Alison. She's as thrown as you. With what Wren did to her… Ryan had to wade across a lot of minefields to build something with your mom because of him. I swear, if he was alive today, I'd probably kill him myself for what he did to you, to Jenny."

She'd always known how protective her grandma was.

"Why are you both sitting out here in the cold?" Marcus said as he strode up the steps. He looked over to the door and then down at them, and she didn't miss the fact that he still had his duty belt on, his sheriff's jacket. He was likely stopping just to check in before heading right back to the station.

She pulled in a breath, welcoming the cold. "Didn't much want to talk to anyone. So what happened with Bennett? Did he confess? Is he not only a killer but also the type of crazed sicko only I can attract?"

Her uncle didn't pull his gaze from her at first. When he did, his wince didn't make her feel better. It made her feel worse. "I'm so sorry," he said. "I wish I could say something to make this better for you. I don't know how to get you to understand this, kiddo, but it isn't you. Beating yourself up, Alison…" He lifted his hand and then dropped it as if at a loss for words.

"So where is Harold?" Iris asked.

Marcus dragged his gaze over to her and pulled in a breath. "At the station. The crime scene techs wrapped up at Belinda's, but we're feeling stretched pretty thin, trying to tie this all up. I left Harold with Bennett. Haven't been able to charge him yet, and we haven't gotten a warrant to get back in his place." He stopped talking, and she knew there was something he wasn't saying. "He hasn't confessed. He denies any involvement in what happened to Chad, Hunter, Amanda, Belinda, and Cassie. In fact, he's been pretty convincing, and without that list of yours, that missing page…"

Her hands were fisted in her down jacket. "Is he really Wren's son?" she said. Out of everything, that one question was the one she wanted—no, needed to know the answer to.

Marcus had an expression she'd seen a time or two when things were really bad. She wondered whether he'd brush her off and not tell her.

"Please don't lie to me," she said. "Growing up with Wren, I always knew he was hiding something. He was a complicated man who manipulated my mother. He was cruel. He took pleasure in hurting her and then building her up again. He was sick and twisted, yet I knew he loved me. He'd never give a straight answer. Secrets and lies… Please be straight with me. If anything, I think I'm owed that. Aside from this situation with Wren and Bennett, I know someone read my very private thoughts, that list. I mean, why did Bennett have those photos of me, of my mom? Why was he so interested in me? You know, the first time I met him, he was in the restaurant. He saw when Chad put his hand on me and I told him to take it off. He was in my corner even when Chad pulled that dickhead move and said it was nothing, giving some excuse, saying I was making too much of it. Bennett called him out to me. I kind of need to know, because none of this makes sense…" She stopped talking.

"Alison is right, Marcus," Iris said. "She needs to know. We all do."

Marcus was looking at her grandma. The gaze lingered more than a moment, and then he nodded only once. "Fair enough. Bennett Warren is the son of Wren Sweetgrass and Lizzie Warren. We ran his ID. He grew up in Idaho, Boise, with his mother."

"Let me guess," she said, cutting him off. "He's not a med student?"

He raised a brow and made a face. "Actually, he is. What we can't figure out is why he was watching you. Was he following you? What, exactly, were his reasons? We don't know, and he's not talking. I'm not objective when it comes to you, so Harold is there. We've asked him about the page from your journal. He keeps denying it, says he's been in your apartment only the time you invited him over. He keeps denying the journal, the assaults, the murder. He said he doesn't know who these people are. We need a warrant to get back into his place, because right now, because of how we got in, the photos on the wall won't be admissible in court."

"But he's still in jail?" she said, pulling her hands from her pockets.

Marcus nodded. "For now, yes—but we haven't charged him."

"And will you?"

His blue eyes flickered as he stared down at her. He was listening to her, giving everything to her. He nodded. "It's only a matter of time. After seeing those photos, I have the feeling he's good for it. We'll make sure he's charged and that he pays for what he's done."

CHAPTER

Fifteen

"I still don't think this is a good idea," Jenny said.

The streets were dark, and Alison turned to her mom behind the wheel of her Jeep. Jenny was wearing a dark blue bomber jacket, her long dark hair pulled back in a ponytail, and Alison found herself taking in her mother's hands on the wheel, seeing her dad's ring on her finger as she turned right. It was such a contrast to the ring from Wren. She remembered the large rock, the intricate design, the difference between her mom then and who she was now.

"Look, Uncle Marcus has already said they have Bennett in custody, and I'd rather not sleep on that lumpy pullout in the spare room or on an air mattress on the floor. I have a comfortable bed, my bed, in my apartment. The only reason I was staying over was because we didn't know who was hurting everyone. Now we do, and he's in custody, so I'm going home where I can sleep and have some time to figure out why I always seem to attract this..." She gestured to the window, seeing the streets downtown and the closed restaurant she wasn't sure she still worked at.

"You don't have a corner on bad things happening to you," Jenny said. "I'm so furious over this situation. If I could, I'd take it on for you. No one deserves this. I feel as if I'm responsible…" Her mom lifted a hand and then gripped the wheel again.

She knew how quiet she'd been all night, just like her. A dark cloud seemed to hang over all of them. "Why do you think he did it?"

Her mom signaled and pulled into the parking lot, into an empty spot, and shoved the vehicle in park. The engine was idling. The heat was blowing. "Are we talking about Bennett or someone else?" she said. Her coat rustled against the leather seat, and she turned to Alison, her hand on the shoulder strap of the seat belt.

"Well, Bennett, of course," Alison said. "Did you have any idea Dad had another kid, that he was involved with someone else? Was he even involved with her? I mean, the photos on the wall… Who does that?"

Her mom sighed, then dragged her gaze over to her. "There were a whole bunch of things about Wren that I had no idea about. He was complicated. In case you didn't know, but I'm sure you do, he was into things, dark things, things I never would've wanted you to know about. I suspected certain things about him, and I've spent a lot of nights, hours, time thinking of how I saw it then, the signs and evidence. He was a complex man who was deeply flawed. During that time of my life, I just lived through it with him, the way he spoke to me, the slights, the cruel remarks, the things he did.

"I think back and have asked myself a hundred times, a thousand times, why I didn't see what I see now. I know I'm not really answering, but you have to know that with

Wren, you didn't know something unless he wanted you to. So no, I had no idea about Bennett or his mother. Seeing the photos, I realized Wren had a whole other life that I had no idea about." Her mom lowered her gaze, looking away. "I'm sorry, Alison. I don't even know what to apologize for—Bennett, Wren, your broken heart." When she lifted her gaze again, the anguish she could see there didn't help her feel any better. "Maybe that's why I wish you'd reconsider and stay, move back home for now. I just feel like there's so much I'm responsible for, so much I need to make right, to fix…"

She took in the hedges, the lights of the courtyard, the concrete that had been shoveled of snow and was dry. "Mom, I know I blamed you for a lot, but I also know Wren never treated me like he did you. For a lot of years, I thought you'd done something to deserve the way he talked to you. I think back and remember the way he snapped and the way you took it, the second he could go from warm and laughing to cruel and cutting with you. I never saw him touch you, but his words were like a slap to you. Yet he gave me everything…until that drunken moment when he told me I wasn't his. I hated him for that. I didn't even realize then that I was seeing the underlying hate he had for you. It started to make sense. All those years, all those cruel remarks and put downs, they were his way of punishing you. But why? If he had a son, Bennett, who was his, why didn't he just go to her, be happy with her? That picture of Wren with Bennett's mother on the wall…"

Jenny didn't shake her head, but Alison could see she was at the same loss for words, reliving that time. So many questions and so few answers. Her mom said nothing.

"I just don't understand why he had those photos of us," Alison said. "Did he take them? Was he planning something to hurt us, to get even? Yet everything he said to me was the complete opposite. I swear, as I go over it in my mind, it doesn't make sense."

Her mom reached over and rested her hand on hers, taking it and squeezing it. "Nothing about Wren and who he was makes sense. I've racked my brain, trying to think of what I missed. He wasn't a good man, but he did give the impression of a man who did things. Your dad knows. It took me a while to talk to Ryan about it, but he figured out a lot before. After Wren, when I moved us here, I swore I would never…" Her mom fisted her hand. "I would never again allow a man to treat me as if I was no one. When Ryan showed up on our doorstep, with everything that had happened, no matter how much I wanted him and that something between us, I wasn't ever going to allow another man in. But he waited. He was patient. I knew from the get-go that he wasn't Wren, but sometimes it takes a long time until what you know becomes what you feel deep down. What I now know is that Ryan, your dad, is such a good man. I almost didn't want to take a chance because I believed I couldn't pick a man for the life of me, and Ryan was too good to be true, so he would suddenly have a dark side that I didn't see. I understand well how the mind messes with you."

She had no idea her mom had been that tormented. "So you almost didn't marry Dad because you thought he could be another Wren?"

Her mom didn't shake her head. The smile that touched her lips seemed so sad as she looked back to her. It was there in her eyes even though it was dark. "No, I pushed your dad away. I wouldn't let him in here." She tapped her heart. "But he didn't go away. When I pushed, I realized he was waiting me out because he believed in us. What I'm saying is that your special guy will just be there one day, suddenly. You'll find him or he'll find you, but until then, we have a family. They really love you and would do anything for you. As far as Bennett, I don't know what to say about him. What could possibly have been going through his mind? How long has he been watching you, me, and Wren? What did he want? I only hope Marcus and Harold figure it out, get the answers, because I know your dad likely won't rest until they do. At the same time, he's going to be angry that you're here, wanting to stay at your place. I'll explain it to him, because I get it, just wanting space."

She realized her mom really did understand her.

Alison reached for the door handle and slipped out of the Jeep, reaching for the bag her dad had made her pack to stay over. She slipped it over her shoulder and took in her mom, who didn't unfasten her seatbelt.

"Alison," Jenny called out, "if you change your mind as soon as you get up there, call me. I'll come back for you."

She hesitated only a second. "Mom, don't worry. I'm fine, and thanks for…" She stopped. This wasn't her. Being touchy-feely and sharing with her mom was something she didn't do. "Sorry for being so hard on you. I'll call you tomorrow."

Then she closed the door before her mom could say anything else, stepping up onto the sidewalk and feeling the cold. She heard her mom back out and pulled in a breath, looking forward to having time alone by herself without anyone looking over her shoulder or questioning her. She wanted a hot bath, a cup of tea, and then to crawl into bed and sleep.

As she looked up, she froze. The jolt of fear made her breath catch as she saw the darkness of her window.

"Stupid, stupid!" How could she have left without checking? She never turned it off at night, She had to remind herself, as she stood there, staring, that she had left hours ago, in the light of day. Someone in her family must have shut it off.

Her heart thudded, and she forced herself to take one step and then another. "Now you're just being paranoid," she said as she reached the faint light of the stairs and started up, her bag over her shoulder, her hand in her pocket, over her keys.

She hurried up and stopped at the top, seeing her door and Bennett's. She had to remind herself he was in jail. She shoved her key in the lock and turned it, hearing the click, feeling the panic of being out in the hall with that creepy feeling that went up her back, and she stepped inside and flicked the light. She closed the door, flicked the lock and the chain, and stepped inside.

Her stomach bottomed out.

"Well, hello there," Dax said.

She didn't know why, but it was his beard she noticed first: bright red. He leaned forward in the chair, and her journal was lying open on the sofa table in front of him. Her ears were ringing over the sound of her breath, echoing, surreal.

He gestured wide and went to stand, and she took in his striped T-shirt and sweatpants, his socks, as if he'd made himself at home. "Come on, Alison. Come on over here and sit." He patted the sofa.

She knew where the door was behind her, and she squeezed the strap of her bag as she realized her phone was ringing.

"Oh, no, don't go answering that. Come on over here and sit down." He sounded so damn friendly when this was anything but.

"How did you get into my apartment, Dax? Why are

you in here?" She was staring at her journal. Bennett was in jail. This was all wrong.

"Well, you wouldn't believe the number of keys floating around in an apartment complex. If anyone really knew how many strangers have keys to their places…" He didn't smile, but he did pat the sofa again and gestured to her book.

She didn't want to move. Her phone stopped ringing, and she glanced down to her pocket. What would he do if she ran to the door?

"So it was you in my apartment, reading my journal. The list of names…" she started.

He angled his head and reached for an orange soda that must have been in her fridge. "I'm sure you're thinking this is weird, and I can tell by your face that you're freaking out, but just hear me out, please. Come and sit." He was standing again.

She took in his arms, the size of them, and reached in her pocket just as her phone started ringing again. She put her bag down, unable to stop the trembling, and took a step. When she pulled out her phone, she saw her dad's name on the screen. Why the hell hadn't she listened?

Dax was over in two steps and took the phone from her hand. "I asked you nicely, Alison. After what I did for you, please show me some respect." He looked at the screen and shook his head. "Your dad is calling, but you can't talk to him right now. Come on, sit. Sit."

She looked over to the door, knowing it was locked, and counted in her head how long it would take her to get there and open it. He'd be right on top of her. She'd never get out.

"I asked you to sit nicely, and I mean it, Alison. We need to talk. I need you to explain something to me." He was still gesturing to the sofa.

She took one step and then another, then sat on the edge, at the far end, and fisted her hands. She had always thought his eyes were blue, but they were actually hazel. Just another thing she thought she'd known that had been a lie.

"Were you the one who hurt Chad?" she said.

He was sitting on a dining chair now, one of his hands on his knee, resting on it. Her phone, which was now on the sofa table in front of him, lit up again, and she could see *Dad* on the screen.

"Your dad really is annoying, isn't he?" Dax said. "I didn't see him on your list, but we could add him, you know."

Her heart thudded long and loud. "Not my dad," she said. "And you didn't answer me about Chad."

He glanced to the phone, which had finally stopped after three rings, going to voicemail again. "He really was an asshole. You were right to put him on your list. The way he treated you… Belinda, he liked her. He always ridiculed me, too. Kept calling me 'big boy' even though I asked him to stop. He said he didn't want to waste the extra pay to fire you, you know. He joked about making things so difficult that you would finally quit. I should have hit him harder. I reached for a rolling pin when he turned his back. Everyone was gone, putting away the food, and I just hit him. Thought he was dead. I dragged his body behind the lettuce crates."

Her hand was on her chest. She was horrified by what he'd said, but at least she knew she wasn't going crazy. Chad had been trying to force her out. She shook her head. "And Hunter, Amanda, Belinda…?"

He reached into his pocket and unfolded the page, the list of names from her journal. "You're a very angry young lady, Alison. After reading this…" He lifted the book. "My heart was breaking for you. What those kids at high school did to you... They're a spoiled bunch. They thought nothing of throwing you under the bus. How easy it is to scapegoat someone. I know all too well what that feels like, Alison. Hunter was one lucky son of a bitch. I followed him, and when he got out of his car, I floored it and hit him. He flew. No one could've been more surprised than me that he survived, but he did. With Amanda, the gas leak would've been perfect. I didn't count on her neighbor coming over.

"When it comes to planning the perfect crime, you hear about killers who make mistakes early on and then get better. By the time it was Belinda's turn, I was ready. She really was a pretty thing, but I saw the way she looked at you when you weren't looking. She wasn't a nice girl. Belinda left the back door open. You have any idea how many people don't lock their doors when they're home? I just walked in. She was upstairs, running the bath, and no one was home. I waited until the water stopped and I heard her get in. She had the bathroom door ajar, and I peeked in. She had her eyes closed, leaning back, listening to music with earbuds in. I just walked right up to her, put my hand on the top of her head, and pushed her under and held her down. Oh, she fought. She was strong. She even got me good with her nails." He lifted his arm to show the scabbed-over scrape where she had clawed him.

Alison pulled in one breath and then another. *Just breathe!*

"I'm sorry I didn't follow the list in order," he said. "Just one question, Alison. Cassie, you crossed her out, yet you circled her name again. I wanted to ask you about that." He was holding the list.

She stared in horror, wondering why she'd never seen that Dax was absolutely crazy—yet he sounded so sane.

Her phone started ringing again, and this time she could see Marcus's name. Dax grabbed the phone and roared, throwing it with a sweep of his hand to the wall, where it shattered. She shrieked.

The door burst open, and it happened so fast, the commotion. She was grabbed by her dad, and Marcus had his gun out, and Harold was there too. They had Dax on the ground. There was yelling, and she was shaking as her dad held her close in his arms, turning her away so she couldn't see. But she could still hear the rambling craziness of a man she'd worked with, had liked. She realized she'd known absolutely nothing about him.

And what about Bennett? Now she was more confused than ever.

CHAPTER
Sixteen

"That's not how you polish a glass or fold a napkin," Suzanne said. Her hair was hanging long and loose, and she was in flats. "Come on, Alison. One, two, three. Easy, see?"

Alison took in the gymnasium, where red and white balloons hung on the wall alongside a big *Congratulations, Sheriff!* banner that had been colored by Eva. It had been missing the final *f* until Jenny grabbed a pen and filled it in. It was priceless.

Alison would've taken more enjoyment out of it if she hadn't been wallowing.

"Come on," Suzanne said. "I'm done half the napkins, but you've been working on the same one for the last ten minutes."

Alison took in the rolls of paper towel Owen had dropped off. Their election night party was on a budget, so ripping off pieces and folding them into napkins was what she'd been reduced to, along with polishing the dusty, streaked glasses her dad had carried in.

"Sorry," was all she could say.

It seemed for the past week that this was all Suzanne had done, driving up to the house and dragging her around everywhere with her, shopping, getting her nails and hair done, baking, and taking walks she didn't want to take.

"You know, that's all I've heard from you," Suzanne said. "We all get it, Alison. You're sorry, but we're sorry more. Everything is done, over. Dax is in jail, and you're back home, where you should be. Ryan and Jenny are breathing easier, and you're going to be okay. I'll keep telling you every day if you like. And your grandma and what's his face are sticking around a bit longer for you."

She knew what's his face was Raymond, a.k.a. Jake. Suzanne was still getting her head around calling him that.

She'd heard the speech already, every day. Don't worry, don't be sorry, it's over.

But it wasn't over, not in her mind. She didn't think she'd ever get past the horror of walking into her darkened apartment to find Dax sitting there. He'd read her journal, stolen the ripped-out page. He'd gone through her things, been in her apartment, been watching her from the sidelines since she started at the restaurant. But who could have known that his father was one of six owners of the Carlyle, each of whom had a set of keys to all the units?

She wasn't sure she'd ever feel safe again after hearing that he'd made a game of picking apartments and sneaking in, going through people's things. He'd read her journal.

"Suzanne, I appreciate it, and I know it's important to be here for Marcus tonight if he wins, but..."

"Excuse me! *When* he wins," Suzanne cut in. "Have some faith, Alison. Marcus is going to win this election as sheriff, because the alternative is Lonnie, and that would be absolutely the worst thing for this town. He's a bottom feeder, and the people here know it."

Alison looked around, seeing her grandparents across the room, and Owen and Tessa. Even Luke was back, over with Brady and Cassie, who still wore a cast and a sling. Karen and Jack were also hustling around with the volunteers and others who wanted Marcus re-elected.

Yet she couldn't help feeling as if she'd be the reason he wouldn't win.

"You really think he's going to win with everyone knowing about my 'kill list' or the fact that I'm the sheriff's fucked-up niece? Because I don't."

"You're not fucked up, Alison," Suzanne said.

"Really? That's not what Lonnie said."

She didn't think she'd ever forget the news conference, the way Lonnie had exposed her journal, held up the page with the list of names. Brady and Cassie would never have known otherwise.

"Lonnie's an asshole. We've already covered that," Suzanne said.

Alison knew she should've stayed home, but her mom and dad wouldn't hear of it. It seemed everyone was making her do things of late so she wouldn't get stuck in her misery.

"He's a piece of shit," Suzanne continued. "He took evidence from a crime scene and used it to discredit Marcus. You were a casualty. People will see him as the pariah he is, and when Marcus wins this election, the first thing he's going to do is have Lonnie drawn up on charges and fired, city council be damned. Those were his exact words. You forget, Alison, that none of us takes kindly to what he did. Your dad... I shouldn't be telling you this." Suzanne turned her back to the table and leaned against it, her arms crossed, right beside Alison. "Your dad had a gun in Lonnie's face. He'd cocked it, too, and was going to pull the trigger if Marcus and Harold hadn't pulled him off." She shrugged. "With what he did, hurting you and all of us, we're out for blood."

She looked over to her parents, who were talking to a volunteer. They were both dressed in their fancy clothes, their Sunday best.

Then there was Brady, who she knew would never forgive her.

The hate in his eyes when he'd heard… She knew that was the end for them. Cassie, too, she was sure. Her heart still ached over that.

"You should go and talk to him." Suzanne poked her, and she realized she knew she was staring right at Brady.

"No! It's bad enough you made me come, but I'm not going over there. I get it. They hate me. They have every right." She reached for a paper towel and took in her aunt, who seemed to be her only friend. "Leave it alone, please, for my sake."

Suzanne only shrugged. "I heard Bennett reached out to you."

She lifted her gaze across the room, seeing her dad laughing about something, his arm around her mom. It was her dad who hadn't been able to let the Bennett thing drop. The night her uncle had broken down her apartment door, it was because Bennett had walked when his lawyer arrived, and she hadn't been answering her phone. They'd feared the worst.

But they'd all been shocked to learn it was Dax. Every one of them was still trying to understand how this could happen. That night was the first time she'd been so happy for the O'Connell overprotectiveness.

"Yeah, well, it's not going to happen. Turns out he wasn't the crazy sicko I thought he was. He was just Wren's son, who'd been watching me and my mom from a distance, taking pictures of us. I still have no idea what he was planning on doing. I should be creeped out, but instead I don't know what to feel."

She heard cheering and yelling, then saw Marcus and Charlotte with Eva and Cameron, walking in amid congratulations.

So he had won. She knew she should be happy, and she tried to tell herself she was.

"Alison, hey."

She nearly jumped out of her skin as she turned to see Bennett, tall, dark, and charming, walking her way.

Suzanne rested a hand on her arm and said, "Glad you could come, Bennett. Why don't I leave you two to talk?"

Then she stepped away, and all Alison could do was stare at her back. Everyone was congratulating her uncle and caught up in the celebration of the moment. She didn't have a clue what to say as she took in the sadness in the way Bennett looked at her with those eyes, which she now knew were Wren's.

"Did your dad tell you I came by to see you?" he said.

She just looked at him, not knowing what to say. "He said you reached out to me, but honestly, I don't know why, after everything that happened. If it's all the same to you, I feel bad enough over everything and what I did. I don't want to have to say sorry to one more person."

He nodded and took another step closer until he was standing right in front of her. "I get it, I really do, but in all fairness, Alison, I need you to hear me out. I like you. I guess I can understand how you may have taken what you saw the wrong way. I already talked to your dad, to your mom, and they both said it would be better if you and I talked face to face. So that's all this is, Alison. But if you tell me to get lost, I will."

She squeezed the napkin and pulled in a breath, but she couldn't get the words out.

He stepped back and lifted his hands in resignation. "Okay, I get it," he said. "I won't bother you again."

And she watched him walk away.

Seventeen

He wasn't a bad guy, he knew that. There was something uncomfortable about realizing Alison had a different perspective of him now, that she believed something without knowing the entire story.

"Bennett, wait!"

The parking lot was full. He turned around in the snow, taking in Alison slipping in her ridiculously high heels. She wore a red low-cut shirt and a black skirt that was made for the summer. He took a step away from his car, watching the ridiculous way she walked.

"You realize you're wearing the wrong shoes for this weather?" he called out. "You're going to fall on your ass. Just stay where you are."

As he walked toward her, he passed others heading toward the school auditorium. He knew her uncle was now the elected sheriff, and he still wasn't sure how to feel about that. Hurt was hurt. They'd treated him as if he were guilty, looking at him in a way he didn't believe he'd ever forget. He looked down as he walked, stepping over ice and snow. Alison was standing, waiting, and she had to be freezing.

"I'm sorry I was such a bitch in there," she said. "It seems everyone is angry at me, and I just want to hide, but no one will let me, so this is what you get."

He took in the heavy shadow and liner, the sadness that seemed to linger in her expression. He stopped in front of her and shrugged off his wool coat. "Here, you're not even dressed properly. You're going to freeze." He settled it over her shoulders and touched her arm, then helped her over to the side. His black knit shirt did nothing to ward off the chill. "So you're chasing me down, now."

She didn't smile, her jaw set.

"Look, Alison, I don't know why anyone would be angry with you. I'm not."

She looked up and then away. He was familiar with how it felt to be just plain hurting, and that was exactly what he was seeing in this girl, whom he'd never expected to like the way he did.

"Well, I'm responsible for this mess. My dad said you got kicked out of your apartment. A girl is dead, and others are hurt just because I wrote their names in a book. Bennett, I feel like I've had the shit kicked out of me. I lost my job, too. I don't know what to say. Yeah, my mom and dad said you came by. I even heard you, but what am I supposed to say? I attract this. I'm still trying to make sense of why Dax, just a cook I had no issues with, suddenly became obsessed with me. Like, who does that?"

He didn't know what to say as he pulled in a breath, taking in this girl who was so complicated. Everything had gone so well until it hadn't.

"What happened to you isn't okay," he said. "But you should know how angry I am with your uncles, Marcus and Harold, for how they treated me. I seriously thought I was going to be railroaded. They had enough to spin a story that would've ended with me dying in prison. It's humbling and terrifying to realize how easy it is. So, yeah, I get that you're angry. I am, too. But you need to understand about the photos. That's why I'm here. I already talked to Jenny and Ryan."

She looked up to him slowly, as if she didn't want to know. "So Wren is your father? I don't know what to say. All the photos you had of me, of my mom, of Wren… That woman he was with, she was your mother?"

What was he supposed to say about a man he'd never met? The chance to meet him had been stolen from him. That photo had been in his mother's things.

He pulled in a breath and took in the girl who had been raised by a man he'd never been able to get from his mind. He'd been cheated.

"Growing up, I heard about Wren Sweetgrass," he said. "His name is on my birth certificate. That photo with my mom is the only one she had. Did he know about me? According to my mom, he did, but I never understood why he didn't want to meet me. My mother never spoke of him again after my eighth birthday. Whatever happened, I don't know."

The way she was looking at him, he didn't know what she was going to say.

"Your mom told me about Wren," he said, "how he was, what he did to you. Ryan told me some of the things he found out, but he didn't have to say it. My mother was just a black woman to Wren, a nobody. I don't think he even saw her as a person. The reason I had all those photos was that I was trying to find answers. Do you have any idea what it feels like to not be wanted? I really believe that Wren Sweetgrass saw my mother as nothing but a black woman without a voice."

She still said nothing, and he wondered if she had any idea of the things he'd learned about the man he shared blood with: powerful, privileged, a monster.

"So you weren't stalking me?" she said.

He knew that was how they'd seen it, and he supposed they were right, although he was still furious that they'd broken into his apartment, and he wondered why he didn't have the rights he was entitled to. Even after hearing the apology from Marcus, who had stood before him, hat in hand, he was trying to shake the hard feelings that lingered.

"I wasn't stalking you," he said. "When I moved here, though, I knew you and Jenny were here, and I planned on confronting both of you to get the kind of answers that would give me some peace. I never expected you to move in right next door. The pictures were taken by a private investigator I hired to track down everything about Wren. He was a puzzle I was putting together."

"It's creepy," she said, and he wondered if she understood what she was saying.

"And creating a kill list isn't?" he replied.

There it was. She'd taken it the wrong way.

"I'm making a point, Alison, not being cruel," he said. "What you wrote was private and personal, and no one had a right to it. That other guy who was running for sheriff, the way he aired that page publicly crossed so many lines. I seriously don't know how I'd handle anyone reading my personal, private thoughts and putting them out there on the news for everyone. I felt for you, Alison. That's why I took your dad's calls and accepted his apology."

He wasn't sure she was ready to listen. He could see how raw the wound still was.

"So my dad apologized?" she said. "I didn't know that."

He could see people watching them, and he wanted to tell them to mind their own business. "So did Marcus and Harold. I just wasn't ready to accept theirs. Not sure when or if I will be."

"But the photos…" she started.

He could see how creeped out she was and why her dad had insisted he explain it to her. "The photo of Wren and my mom was hers. I'd always known what he looked like. The ones of you and your mom, as I said, were taken by my PI. I was trying to get answers, understand where I came from. I created a timeline, a history, to try to understand why Wren couldn't give me anything, even an acknowledgement of my existence. I always thought it was because of the color of my skin. You tell people that, and they tell you you're crazy, but after growing up in Boise, which is the worst place for someone who looks like me, I started to believe people aren't equal."

Alison looked up at him and knit her brow. "I remember you said your mother died, and you went looking for your father. Is that when you had the photos taken of me and my mom? I didn't know you existed, that Wren had a son. I do know he had a lot of secrets, and he could be a cruel man. I know how he treated my mother. Maybe you and yours should consider yourselves lucky."

"The thing is, Alison, someone telling me to consider myself lucky doesn't help. It doesn't fill that big hole I have. Yeah, your dad explained what happened to Wren, how he died. I get that he wasn't a nice man, but he was my father."

"How did your mother die?" she said. There was something about the way she looked up to him: The spark of light was missing from her eyes, and he wished he could see it again.

"Oh, it wasn't quick. The end was her on a slab in the

morgue, labeled just another junkie on the streets, but that wasn't my mother. She was a bank teller. She suffered a back injury while hauling boxes from an old storage room, which she had no business doing. The metal rack was unstable and came down on her when she pulled one from the top shelf. There was nerve damage, the doctor said. He prescribed her oxy for the pain and said the injury was something she'd have to live with. Then it was the same old story. She was hooked, couldn't work, lost her job. With no more refills, she went to the streets and died with a needle in her arm. It's why I went to med school, because that never should have happened…"

He stopped talking, and he could see she was really thinking. She nodded.

"I'm kind of a mess, you know," she said. "I'm not a nice person, and being seen with me could have you tarred and feathered. As Chad said, I'll never work in this town again. Once everyone heard it was my list, they thought I had planned for all this to happen."

He knew she was gutted, and he still remembered the words her dad had used: *Please. She blames herself. Help her.*

He pulled his arms across his chest and couldn't stop the shiver. She went to pull off his coat, but he stopped her. "Don't you think it's up to me whether I want to be seen with you?" he said. "If it's all the same to you, Alison, I learned a while ago not to pay too much mind to what people think of me, because I'm living my life for myself, not anyone else. Who I'm friends with is my choice."

She shrugged and gestured toward him. "So I'm your friend?"

"Well, I thought we were. Not sure where we are now," he said.

She held her hand out, and he just stared at it, seeing how scared she was.

He took it. "Is this an invite?"

There it was, that saucy, flirty smile that only Alison could give. She flicked her mysterious brown eyes up to him. "A fresh start."

He linked his fingers with hers and started walking carefully as she held on to his arm with her other hand.

"So where are you living now?" she asked.

He realized her dad had never told her. "You mean after the locks were changed on my apartment even though I paid my rent?"

She looked at him as if she knew that his landlord would end up on his own list, one he'd never want made public.

"I spent a couple very cold nights in my car, but there's a really nice condo downtown that your sister owns, apparently. Your dad talked to her and showed up with the keys. It's already furnished. Your uncles somehow managed to get my things from my old place. Is it better? Yes, but how it happened…" He shook his head, taking in the shock in her expression.

"Dad never said anything. Neither did anyone else."

"Well, I figure it was their way of trying to make things right."

She stopped at the door and looked up to him, something else on her mind. "So if I invite you, say, for dinner tomorrow night, what would you say?"

He just took her in, sensing her hesitation. "You mean at your mom and dad's house?"

She had him moving again, holding on to his arm so she wouldn't slip. "Well, actually, tomorrow we're at Marcus's, which is right across the street from my parents' place. It's family night. Everyone will be there. Owen will barbecue, and everyone will be in your business, putting you in the hot seat, but they're nice, and…"

He pulled open the door, and she stopped talking and looked right up to him.

"They're my family, Bennett, and I want you to come," she finally said.

He didn't know what it was about this girl. He felt a pull toward her that he'd never felt with anyone before. "You know what, Alison? That's all I needed to hear. You want me there, I'll be there."

There it was, that smile, that flicker of life in her eyes that made Alison the kind of girl, he realized, that very few would ever really understand.

"I don't think he'll ever forgive me," Alison said.

Eva looked up to her. Her dark hair was tucked under a wool hat, and she wore a pink winter coat. Alison knew her cousin understood far more than anyone gave her credit for. At eight years old, she'd experienced more than a kid should have. At times, she really was the little sister Alison had always wanted.

"Did you say you're sorry?" Eva said. "Because Marcus and Charlotte always say to just say you're sorry. I know Marcus says he's sorry to Charlotte a lot, when he works late, when she gets mad at him. Sometimes I wonder what he did. I asked him once, and he said sometimes you just have to say it when someone is upset, even when you don't know what you did."

Alison found some amusement in the relationship between Marcus and Charlotte. As they walked back across the street from her parents' house to Marcus's, her carrying the tray of veggies her mom had cut up and Eva carrying a container of cookies she'd made, she took in Bennett's white Volvo parked out front.

He was basically cornered at Marcus's, having a one-on-one with Jake, a.k.a. Raymond. The only thing that made the evening worse was the fact that Brady and Cassie had said not two words to her. The tension was almost unbearable.

"Are you going to do it?" Eva asked.

They took their time walking. Everyone was crowded in at Marcus's. Luke was back home, and Karen and Jack were there, too. She was still having trouble with the fact that her dad was responsible for Bennett now living in Karen and Jack's condo.

She thought of all the reasons why saying she was sorry wouldn't work, but she said, "I'll think about it."

Little Eva sighed. "Don't think about it, Alison. Just do it. Just go up and say you're sorry. If you want, I could go with you."

Eva could say all the right things at times, and she cringed inwardly, knowing Eva could never think badly of her. It was that unconditional love she'd never thought existed.

"You'd really go up to Brady and Cassie with me and stand there so I can apologize?"

They were trudging up the cleared walkway to Marcus's, and her heart was now hammering again. She wanted to just pull Bennett aside and talk to him, try to forget about Brady and Cassie, but they were still there, and that tension she felt whenever she knew someone didn't like her lingered.

"Uh-huh," Eva said, sounding so damn happy. "I sure would."

Ahead, the door opened. It was Luke, who must have been watching her. Her uncle, the military hero, had likely heard an earful from Brady already. He let Eva go in first, then stepped out into the cold, blocking her way and letting the door close behind him. The maneuver was planned, she could see. Evidently, he had something to say to her.

"Bennett seems pretty decent," he said. "He could've had quite a chip on his shoulder over what happened, but he seems to be rather gracious. That's another thing in his favor," Luke said.

She stood there in her bomber jacket, holding the tray, as Luke crossed his arms over his impressive chest. In just a T-shirt, he had to be freezing. He looked over her head, something clearly on his mind.

"If you don't mind just saying whatever it is, I'd like to put this tray down inside," she said, "and get back to Bennett before he decides everyone in this family is crazy, puts his coat on, and leaves us for one of the saner families out there."

There it was, that Luke smile, the way he laughed under his breath and flicked his gaze down to her. "You and Brady need to square things away," he said—just one more person telling her to put things right when she didn't know how.

"Eva suggested I say I'm sorry," she said, "but I'm not entirely certain what part to apologize for. I thought something privately and put it to paper because you're not supposed to keep things bottled up. Writing things down is supposed to be therapeutic—and private, or did I forget to mention that?"

His face was a mix of emotions, and he winced and shook his head. "It's a crappy situation. You were screwed, and Lonnie will get his. But never fear, dear girl: I've seen worse. I've already talked to Brady and Cassie, and now it's your turn. We're a family, and you both have to get past this. I could run interference if you like, but I don't think that will solve anything."

Her hands were cold, and Luke finally took the tray from her as if he knew.

"Eva beat you to that," she said. "She already told me to just say I'm sorry. Evidently, she's learned that from Uncle Marcus, who's had plenty of practice with Charlotte. She even offered to walk up to Brady with me for moral support."

Again, Luke offered that odd smile. Something seemed to soften in his eyes at the mention of Eva. "She's a great kid. Seems she's a step ahead of all of us. Maybe I should make her my go-to for advice on my own screwed-up personal life."

She just took in her uncle for a moment, knowing well what he'd given up for the family.

Then the screen door squeaked open, and there was Brady. He was tall, and, with him standing next to Luke, she could see they were brothers in so many ways. Her heart slammed against her chest, and she felt the convergence of several moments she'd being doing her very best to put off forever.

"I'm going to leave you two kids," Luke said as he stepped around Brady and went inside with the tray of vegetables.

For a second, she wished Eva were there as the crutch she'd offered to be.

"So, how are you?" Brady asked, but he pulled his gaze from her as if this was the last place he wanted to be.

"Fine, you?" She cringed inwardly, wishing for once in her life that something inspirational would appear in her brain.

All Brady did was shrug.

"Would it help if I said I'm sorry?" she said.

There it was, the flicker of fire, of passion, as his gaze

landed on her with a punch. There was no fondness left for her. "Why'd you do it?"

"You mean write down my personal thoughts, which were mine and should never have gone any further?"

He didn't nod. She could feel the way he was beginning to pull back. His hands were shoved in his pockets, and his face held a hardness that hadn't been there before. "You wrote down Cassie's name on some sick, twisted hate list."

His words were a slap.

"I was angry because you were so damn happy, and I wasn't," she said. "After what happened to us, I felt as if the rug would always be pulled out from under me. It seemed everyone hated me. Cassie's name… I crossed it out and circled it again because I didn't want to like her. If you had written down your thoughts about people you were angry with and someone found them and went public with them, how would you feel?"

But she knew, as he looked away, that he wasn't about to hear her.

"You know what?" she said. "Forget it."

She started to move past Brady, but the door opened, and there were Cassie and Bennett. Great. This was turning into another three-ring circus.

"We could hear you both out here and figured you may need some referees," Cassie said. Her dark hair, a curly mess, was pulled back, and she had the most amazing smile even though her arm was still in a cast. At least the sling was gone. Alison wondered why she wasn't staring at her with the daggers she should've been.

No one said anything then. Cassie stood right beside Brady, her hand on his arm, whereas Bennett was looking from Alison to Brady as he moved closer to her.

"Cassie and I were just talking about things that

happen in families," he said. "In life, you can decide to hold on to things and not move past them. I mean, out of everyone, I can talk, because I'm here in the sheriff's house despite the fact that Marcus and Harold made my life hell for a moment, with the threats, cuffing me and trying to throw the book at me for something I didn't do. But, believe it or not, Marcus and I just had a civil conversation inside. Alison was violated in a way I can't begin to imagine. So she wrote some angry things. Who doesn't do that? I'm pretty sure she doesn't really hate you, Cassie."

From the way Bennett spoke, she realized he was a skilled negotiator, seeing all sides. For a second, she felt almost as if she could forgive herself.

"Cassie, maybe it's you I should say I'm sorry to," she said. "I am sorry, because I do like you."

Cassie tugged Brady's arm and made a face. "I know that. Brady told me what happened between you, and I can only imagine how awkward it was. Seriously, Brady, enough with the angry glances at Alison. She had some psycho stalking her, in her apartment, going through her things." She looked back to Alison. "I know the diner isn't on the same level as the Bluebird, but there's an opening for a waitress position. It's only part-time, but if you're interested…"

She couldn't believe Cassie was offering to help her.

"It's minimum wage," she continued, "and the tips aren't spectacular, but there's no Chad Hargrave running it. Think about it. If you want it, I'll put in a word for you, and it's yours."

"You'd do that for me?" Alison said.

Cassie made a face. "Of course I would. You're family. Just let me know."

She felt Bennett slide his hand over her shoulder, and she looked up to him. Cassie tugged on Brady again, and they both slipped into the house, which left just her and Bennett. She pulled in another breath.

"Wow, I didn't expect that," she said.

Bennett was in his coat, and for a moment, she had a sinking feeling this was it. He was leaving. He'd had enough. "I like Cassie," he said. "She suggested inside that the four of us do a double date."

She found herself looking to the door and then back to Bennett. "A double date… So does that mean you're not slipping out?"

He let his gaze linger for a minute. Then there it was, that smile. "No, not leaving, even though your family takes quite a bit of getting used to…" He smiled again, teasing.

"Great, so a double date. I suppose you and Cassie already have some ideas?"

His smile widened. "A few. Dinner, movie, and a game night, just the four of us. We'll talk, get to know each other, and you and Brady can let go of this rift."

"You think it'll be that easy?" she asked.

He said nothing for a second. Then he leaned in and kissed her so gently before pulling back. There was something in the way he looked at her so deeply. She realized she might not be so entirely alone as she'd once believed.

"No, but then, if I can walk in here and swallow everything, not holding on to the kind of hate I could, I think you and Brady can get past this."

She considered for only a second what had happened over the past few days, how complex it had all been. Then she held out her hand, and Bennett slid his into hers.

And instead of walking back into the house, he pulled her closer and kissed her again.

Turn the page for a sneak peek of
THE O'CONNELL FAMILY CHRISTMAS coming next in
THE O'CONNELLS
Available in print, eBook & Audio

Next in The O'Connells

THE O'CONNELL FAMILY CHRISTMAS

As Christmas approaches, the O'Connell family's loyalty is tested once again.

Owen O'Connell wants only one thing: to put a ring on the finger of his long-time girlfriend, Tessa Brooks. But when her past fears become an obstacle between them, Owen may not get the new beginning and the happily ever after he truly wants.

Meanwhile, Suzanne O'Connell finds herself in a year-long slump, being the live-in girlfriend of Deputy Harold Waters. Jobless and searching for something to give her life meaning, she finds herself on the wrong side of the law when she stands up for the rights of a stranger who is targeted by the community. Suzanne, who is known for her stubbornness and her obstinate sense of right and wrong, ends up taking on a woman no one else will, and in doing so, she tests her relationship not only with Harold but with every one of the O'Connells.

As the O'Connells work together to keep their sister out of jail, can big brother Owen, who has been a father figure to all his siblings, achieve the future he dreams of with the only woman he's ever truly loved?

As the O'Connells work together to keep their sister out of jail, can big brother Owen, who has been a father figure to all his siblings, achieve the future he dreams of with the only woman he's ever truly loved?

The O'Connell Family Christmas

CHAPTER 1

"I want to get married," Owen said, not pulling his gaze from Tessa, who was holding a chef's knife, chopping peppers on the butcher block island he'd finished installing.

She seemed to freeze, then slowly lifted her eyes to him, still holding a red pepper. Wow, those blue eyes really packed a punch at times. Her frizzled wavy blond hair was in a loose ponytail, and she was wearing one of his T-shirts, the one he'd been looking for, with *Nashville* written across the chest in black.

"And who is it you want to get married to?" she said, lifting a brow and going immediately to teasing, tossing out her edgy, twisty, sarcastic humor. It was her go-to, he had learned well, when she was uncomfortable or when something turned serious.

"…Snow White?" he said. "Seriously, Tessa, you're the only one I'm interested in sleeping with, living with, and being in a relationship with." He slid around and swept his hand across the empty room around them, with only the kitchen table and four chairs. "Come on. You and me, we should get married. You know there isn't anyone else. I'm being serious, here."

He had to fight the urge to laugh at her expression, because there it was again. Her eyes widened, the blue flickering as if she were about to laugh or change the subject, or maybe she was wishing for an interruption so she wouldn't have to answer him.

"And don't do that, there," he said, gesturing between them. "I can see you're freaking out."

"I'm not freaking out, Owen. That's ridiculous. But, seriously, what's the rush? Things are good. Why do you want to go and wreck something that's working perfectly? This thing between us is good, and now you want to mess it up?"

She gestured with the butcher knife, and he found himself staring at it, the way her hand gripped it. She was getting loud, and he could hear the panic cutting into her voice. He pulled his arms across his chest, leaning back on the bar stool at the island, and then reached out and gripped the hand that held the knife. He pulled it from her, and for just a moment, he wasn't sure she'd let it go.

He said not a word, as she seemed to grip it harder. "Tessa, let go. Seriously, I'd rather not be on the receiving end of this with you holding a knife. Come on." He pulled again, and this time she let go and stepped back, slim, sexy, gorgeous—and his, almost. "You know, getting married isn't a death sentence. You're making it seem as if it's the end of the world when it's not. We've been together a long time. Hell, the rest of my family is getting married around me: Ryan, Marcus, even Brady, who's just a kid marrying a kid."

She let out a rude noise and lifted her hands in the air. Then, instead of saying anything more, he watched as she walked out of the kitchen. He could hear her in the hall, then in the bedroom.

"Great, just great, O'Connell," he said under his breath, putting the knife on the island.

He stood up and started out of the kitchen, taking in the small artificial Christmas tree plugged in on the sofa table by the living room window. Striding down the hall, he noted that the wall and trim on one side still needed a coat of paint.

In their bedroom, Tessa was in just a pair of pajama shorts, her back to him, pulling on a bra and fastening it. She reached for a black knit, which she pulled on over her head, and pulled her long hair free from the ponytail.

As he stepped up behind her, their eyes connected in the mirror. "I love you. You know that, right? But you didn't answer me on why this is freaking you out so badly. I knew I'd likely have to do some convincing, but I'm starting to get the feeling you're leaning more towards a no, and I can't help wondering if this is about me."

She looked at him as he set his hands on her shoulders, then over her hair, which needed a good brushing. Then she turned around, resting her hands over his chest, looking up at him. He could feel what a perfect fit she was, but he knew there was something there, some unseen obstacle. He wondered whether she even understood why she instinctively pulled back on so many things. The problem was that for him, it hadn't been a big deal until now.

"Why do you need to get married?" she said. "This is perfect. And why are you suddenly comparing us to your brothers? So what if they get married before us? This isn't a race, you know, and marriage is the kind of institution, frankly, that I equate to people suddenly not having to be on their best behavior, breaking promises, and slowly beginning to hate each other. And let's not forget keeping secrets." She gestured toward him, then pressed her hands to his chest again, running them over it, before letting them fall to her sides.

He couldn't get his head around what she'd just said. Hating each other, keeping secrets? He supposed lying was coming next. He realized, as he stared at her and the mixed emotions staring up at him, that she really believed what she'd said.

"Okay, firstly, that's absolutely crazy thinking, Tessa," he said. "You know I don't have any secrets from you. You know every one of my secrets and every dirty, dark, crazy thing that has happened in my family. What this is about is you and me. I can't believe you're automatically taking a twisted view of how things will be. This has me thinking we're talking about your parents, but we're certainly not Jill and Ted Brooks. They chose to live that lie, that life of broken promises and disappointments, being together, laughing one moment but trash-talking each other behind their backs the next. I mean, seriously, Tessa, I'm pretty sure you would never do that to me, and I can tell you, no matter how angry I get with you sometimes, I'd never cut you up like that. What happens here is between you and me. I'm not going to dissect your character behind your back."

She was so close, and for a moment, he thought she was getting it. She was right there, but she didn't touch him, though he could see she wanted to. Maybe it was the way she was fisting her hands, but he could see the tension in her. He could have just pulled her close and ignored this thing she was feeling and freaking out over. She hated the bickering and back and forth between her parents. It was just one of her quirks, just one of those things that made her who she was.

He'd never realized she was convincing herself that could be them. He hadn't seen that coming.

"This is perfect, what we have," he said. "You're right, but I want to get married. I mean, you're it, and marriage is just me saying there's no one else. You know we're together, and marriage is a natural evolution. We found each other. I love you. We get married, become a family, have kids. I seriously see myself growing old with you, and it excites me, knowing you'd be right there in our old age, racing me down some nursing home hall with a walker, with our grown kids visiting, and our grandkids…"

He had to stop talking, though, because she wasn't smiling. In fact, her frown deepened. Apparently, she wasn't holding on to the same dream he was.

"Then comes the disappointment and broken promises," she said.

Oh, there she went, reverting to that lifetime of hurt she seemed to carry, that pessimism she didn't often express. He wasn't getting through to her.

"I'm not perfect and never pretended to be, Tessa, but we're not your parents. I'll say it again—or do you see us suddenly turning into them?"

She didn't answer, but he could see he'd nailed the deep issue that had her seeing only the worst of relationships.

"I think the conversation we should be having," he continued, "is about your parents and the fact that you've never come to terms with this and who they are. They're flawed deeply, and they have no desire to change. They broke every promise to you, disappointed you, and you figured it was easier to do everything yourself. But you haven't now, not for a while. It's been you and me. I'm pretty sure I'm not your father. I don't understand why you're instantly going there, thinking that could be us. Me putting a ring on your finger, us signing a paper and being mister and missus, that doesn't change who we are. Do you not love me?" He tried to smile, but he could see she wasn't impressed.

"I know we're not my parents, and this isn't about them. Now you're being ridiculous. Of course I love you, or we wouldn't be doing this thing, playing house. But what's the rush?" She shrugged, and he could see she wasn't about to shake this twisted view.

"The rush! You're kidding, right? Tessa, we've been living together for over a year—eighteen months, to be exact. The fact is that I wasn't in a hurry either, but you seem to have your standards set so high that no one can meet them. What exactly is it that you expect is going to happen? Am I suddenly going to turn into someone different, like your dad?"

He leaned in, and by the way she flinched, he knew he'd nailed it, that sore spot of hers. For a moment, he wondered if she'd snarl, and he stepped back, lifting his hands in the air, as she pulled her arms around her chest.

"You know who I am, Tessa. I'm not perfect, not by a longshot, but you know things about me I'd never share with anyone. Or is that the problem?"

She looked over to him so sharply, so fast, her blue eyes flashing. "No, Owen, it's not, and you know that. You know I won't do secrets. I get what happened to you and your family, and I'm just as much a part of it as you are now."

He only nodded as he stepped back, his hands fisted at his sides. He ran one over his hair, letting out a sigh.

She didn't pull her gaze. "You know marriage isn't the answer to everything," she said, and she sounded so reasonable. "What's your hurry, Owen? Why now?"

Again, her voice was so soft, and for a moment, he had to wonder if she wasn't right.

"Because, Tessa, I love you, and I want to have kids, our kids. To me, marriage doesn't seem like the worst thing ever. Maybe I want to tell everyone you're my wife, to just take that next step with you. But I can see from all this that you're not where I am. I have to ask, will you ever be ready, or is it just me you won't marry? I want you to think about it, really, objectively, without your parents' baggage coming into play. Just leave them out of this thing between you and me. Can you do that?"

She jutted her chin and pulled her gaze, and he could see how tense she was. Wow! Just talking about marriage had sent her into a tailspin. Then she shrugged and uncrossed her arms, dragging her gaze back over to him.

Instead of answering, all she did was nod. "I need to get dressed. Can you pack up the vegetables I cut? I promised your mom and Charlotte we'd also bring dessert, which is in the fridge—some pudding for the kids."

As he watched this woman he loved pull on a pair of jeans and run a brush through her hair, he realized she had already shifted her focus to any conversation that didn't include marriage or a future with him.

About the Author

"Lorhainne Eckhart is one of my go to authors when I want a guaranteed good book. So many twists and turns, but also so much love and such a strong sense of family."

(LORA W., REVIEWER)

New York Times & USA Today bestseller Lorhainne Eckhart is best known for writing Raw Relatable Real Romance where "Morals and family are running themes." As one fan calls her, she is the "Queen of the family saga." (aherman) writing "the ups and downs of what goes on within a family but also with some suspense, angst and of course a bit of romance thrown in for good measure." Follow Lorhainne on Bookbub to receive alerts on New Releases and Sales and join her mailing list at Lorhainne-Eckhart.com for her Monday Blog, all book news, giveaways and FREE reads. With over 120 books, audiobooks, and multiple series published and available at all, retailers now translated into six languages. She is a multiple recipient of the Readers' Favorite Award for Suspense and Romance, and lives in the Pacific Northwest on an island, is the mother of three, her oldest has autism and she is an advocate for never giving up on your dreams.

"Lorhainne Eckhart has this uncanny way of just hitting the spot every time with her books."

(CAROLINE L., REVIEWER)

The O'Connells: *The O'Connells of Livingston, Montana are not your typical family. A riveting collection of stories surrounding the ups and downs of what goes on within a family but also with some suspense, angst and of course a bit of romance thrown in for good measure. "I thought I loved the Friessens, but I absolutely adore the O'Connell's. Each and every book has different genres of stories, but the one thing in common is how she is able to wrap it around the family, which is the heart of each story." (C. Logue)*

The Friessens: *An emotional big family romance series, the Friessen family siblings find their relationships tested, lay their hearts on the line, and discover lasting love! "Lorhainne Eckhart is one of my go to authors when I want a guaranteed good book. So many twists and turns, but also so much love and such a strong sense of family." (Lora W., Reviewer)*

The Parker Sisters: *The Parker Sisters are a close-knit family, and like any other family they have their ups and downs. Eckhart has crafted another intense family drama… "The character development is outstanding, and the emotional investment is high…" (Aherman, Reviewer)*

The McCabe Brothers: *Join the five McCabe siblings on their journeys to the dark and dangerous side of love! An intense, exhilarating collection of romantic thrillers you won't want to miss. — "Eckhart has a new series that is definitely worth the read. The queen of the family saga started this series with a spin-off of her wildly successful Friessen series." From a Readers' Favorite award—winning author and "queen of the family saga" (Aherman)*

Billy Jo McCabe Mystery: *The social worker and the cop, an unlikely couple drawn together on a small, secluded Pacific Northwest island where nothing is as it seems. Protecting the innocent comes at a cost, and what seems to be a sleepy, quiet town is anything but.*

Lorhainne loves to hear from her readers! You can connect with me at:

www.LorhainneEckhart.com
lorhainneeckhart.le@gmail.com

facebook.com/AuthorLorhainneEckhart
twitter.com/LEckhart
instagram.com/lorhainneeckhart
bookbub.com/profile/lorhainne-eckhart
pinterest.com/lorhainneeckhart

In the Charm
Unexpected Consequences
It Was Always You
The First Time I Saw You
Welcome to My Arms
Welcome to Boston
I'll Always Love You
Ground Rules
A Reason to Breathe
You Are My Everything
Anything For You
The Homecoming
Stay Away From My Daughter
The Bad Boy
A Place of Our Own
The Visitor
All About Devon
Long Past Dawn
How to Heal a Heart
Keep Me In Your Heart

The O'Connells
The Neighbor
The Third Call
The Secret Husband
The Quiet Day
The Commitment
The Missing Father
The Hometown Hero
Justice
The Family Secret
The Fallen O'Connell
The Return of the O'Connells
And The She Was Gone

The Stalker
The O'Connell Family Christmas
The Girl Next Door
Broken Promises
The Gatekeeper
The Hunted

The Street Fighter
Finding Home

The McCabe Brothers
Don't Stop Me (Vic)
Don't Catch Me (Chase)
Don't Run From Me (Aaron)
Don't Hide From Me (Luc)
Don't Leave Me (Claudia)
Out of Time

A Billy Jo McCabe Mystery
Nothing As it Seems
Hiding in Plain Sight
The Cold Case
The Trap
Above the Law
The Stranger at the Door
The Children
The Last Stand
The Charity
The Sacrifice

The Wilde Brothers
The One (Joe and Margaret)
The Honeymoon, A Wilde Brothers Short
Friendly Fire (Logan and Julia)

Not Quite Married, A Wilde Brothers Short
A Matter of Trust (Ben and Carrie)
The Reckoning, A Wilde Brothers Christmas
Traded (Jake)
Unforgiven (Samuel)
The Holiday Bride

Married in Montana
His Promise
Love's Promise
A Promise of Forever

The Parker Sisters
Thrill of the Chase
The Dating Game
Play Hard to Get
What We Can't Have
Go Your Own Way
A June Wedding

Kate & Walker
One Night
Edge of Night
Last Night

Walk the Right Road Series
The Choice
Lost and Found
Merkaba
Bounty
Blown Away: The Final Chapter
He Came Back

The Saved Series

Saved
Vanished
Captured

Single Titles
Loving Christine

www.ingramcontent.com/pod-product-compliance
Lightning Source LLC
Chambersburg PA
CBHW030959210726
48290CB00007B/2391